REFUSING TO Expire

Tricia Daniels

Dedication

For Jennifer, who lost both her father and her soul mate within a few weeks of each other.

Profound is the word that best describes the strength of a woman who experiences such a loss. In this tragic time of loss and reflection, I'm reminded of an important message that I hope to pass on to my children and grandchildren. Laugh often and live passionately. Practice forgiveness, patience, and kindness. Live your life so you have no regrets. Most importantly, LOVE deeply, for life is precious and we never know how much time we have left with the ones we love.

Our thoughts and prayers are with your family. There is little we can do, other than offer to listen when you need to talk; offer our time when you need a hug; and during the times when you feel that you're all alone in this world, we'll be the gentle reminder that you are loved.

For my friends, old and new, thank you for keeping me grounded; loving me when I feel unlovable, and forgiving me when I screw up.

Especially for my family, and the siblings that I would choose: Angie, Karen, Ren, Jackie, and Catherine. I can't imagine my life without you.

To Gary, the love of my life…I will never take your patience, support, and love for granted. I'm looking forward to a lifetime of endless comic material and your special kind of *sweep me off my feet* romance. What took you so long to find me?

Disclaimer:

This book is a work of fiction. All characters, places, and events are from the author's imagination and should not be confused with fact. Any resemblance to persons, living or dead, events or places, is purely coincidental.

Acknowledgements:

Editing by Karen Hrdlicka of Barren Acres Editing
Cover by Kate Reedwood

Special thank you to the town of Orangeville, the town of Thornbury, The Royal Harbour Resort, Nashville North in Norval, The Cape Rey, Carlsbad Hilton and all of Dufferin County for the endless inspiration for romance in this novel.

All Rights Reserved

This literary work may not be reproduced or transmitted in any form or by any means, including electronic or photographic reproduction, in whole or in part, without express written permission.

The unauthorized reproduction or distribution of this copyrighted work is illegal. Criminal copyright infringement, including infringement without monetary gain, is punishable by law.

Chapter One

Here we go again. That awkward moment of silence where neither of us can think of something to say. He had lots to say when we were chatting online. Things are always different on the other side of a computer screen. People are braver; they're more secure there. We've only been here for an hour, but I already know that I'm never going to hear from him again. Why should he go through the uncomfortable process of telling me that he isn't interested? It's easier to block and *unfriend.*

That seems to be the norm for me these days. Someone initiates a conversation, and I do my best to keep things interesting, but it all comes to a crashing halt eventually. They stop texting, phone calls go unanswered, and profiles simply disappear like magic. They've moved on to better things, I assume, trying not to let it bother me. Obviously, they weren't *the one.* To be honest, it doesn't do much to settle a girl's insecurities; especially when that girl has always been made to feel like she's unworthy of love...and even more so when that girl is *me*.

I glance across the table and watch as he uses his fingers to pick a piece of meat out of his teeth. Ugh. How charming is that? My father always said I tended to be a little too *formal*, but there's something to be said for common manners. Right now, saying goodbye can't come soon enough for me. Why prolong the inevitable? My mind wanders and I wonder what Henry, the teacher, is doing tonight. Now *he* has potential. To me, there's nothing sexier than an intelligent man. The fact that he has bulging biceps doesn't hurt either. At least there's an attraction there, on both sides.

The waitress drops the bill down on the table, pulling me back into the present conversation.

"It was really nice to meet you in person, dear," he says, waiting for me to reach for the bill. "Thank you for meeting me."

Dear? Now that's interesting. It suddenly dawns on me that my current companion hasn't used my name all night. "So, Darren. We've been talking online and texting for several weeks now."

He looks at me curiously, wondering where the conversation is going. "Yes."

"Do you have any clue what my name is?"

"Of course, I know your name," he says defensively. "It's Veronica."

"Nope." I purse my lips and pause a moment, not sure myself how I'm going to react. "My name is Victoria." Surprisingly, I let out a small laugh. It's really not funny at all.

His face turns red as his eyes skirt around the room, avoiding me. I shake my head in disbelief as I get to my feet.

"He could have at least paid," I grumble, on the way back to the car. I check for messages before I leave the parking lot and frown. I begin to back up, then hit the brake and pause before slowly inching my way back into the spot. I promised myself that I would never do the *needy chick* thing, but here I am. I pick up my phone and quickly type,

Tori: Thinking about you.

I instantly regret my decision as I hit send, then drop my cell on the seat beside me.

Henry: Oh? What are you thinking?

I smile.

Tori: What are you up to?
Henry: Just finished marking some papers. What are you wearing? Do you look pretty for Daddy tonight?

Hmmmm. That's new. I do like a dominant man in the bedroom, but I'm not sure I could tolerate the *Daddy Dom* type. At the end of the day, I'm a grown-ass woman, and I don't want to be treated like a child. I struggle with the decision for a few moments, then decide that I don't want to be alone for the rest of my life, so I'll play along for now.

Tori: Yes, Daddy, I'm wearing a new dress just for you.
Henry: Are you wearing panties?
Tori: Yes
Henry: Take them off. Daddy likes it when his little girl doesn't wear panties.

I stare at the phone, feeling well beyond my comfort level. Glancing around the parking lot, I consider it. A young couple laughs loudly, as they make their way to their car, and it makes me nervous. I don't think I can do this. Sadly, this isn't my first rodeo, so I know if I don't, he'll lose interest. I sigh and decide to give him a little white lie.

Tori: I took them off.
Henry: Good girl.

I cringe. Those words make me feel a little creepy. I'm not usually the dominant one in a relationship, but it occurs to me that Henry likes his women *completely* submissive.

♥

Monday evening, I pull into the parking lot of the local Tim Hortons and begin to feel nervous. I quickly flip down the visor and check my makeup in the mirror. I can see Henry already waiting for me inside. Damn, he's hotter than I remembered. I straighten my dress as I walk toward the door.

He raises his head and makes eye contact briefly before looking back down at his phone.

"Hi." I stand at the table, waiting for his acknowledgement.

He finishes typing before he looks up at me. "Hi." Leaning back in his chair, he looks me over thoroughly, before placing his phone face down, on the table.

"I hope you haven't been waiting too long."

"A little while," he says, looking at his watch. "I came straight from work. There wasn't much point in going home first."

I notice he's already bought himself a coffee. "Well, it's really nice to see you again. I'll just grab a tea and be right back." I pause a moment, thinking he may get one for me, but the offer never happens. I'm not more than a foot away from the table before he picks up his phone and busies himself with incoming messages again.

I glance at him a few times while I'm waiting in line, hoping to catch him looking back at me. I spent hours stressing over the perfect dress to wear, but he's more occupied with what's happening on his phone. I try to push aside the disappointment by giving myself a little pep talk. The evening has just begun, so I'm going to do my best to turn things around.

While I wait for my tea, I discreetly try to adjust my boobs. On my way back to the table, I strut my stuff, as best as a woman my age can. I try to hide the pain that shoots to my knees with every step in my three-inch heels. Ugh. The meds I'm taking for the damaged nerves in my leg don't seem to be doing anything, except giving me nightmares, these days. That, and I'm just getting too old for this shit.

My stomach flutters when he looks up and locks his eyes to mine. Well, he's looking at my boobs, but I'll take it. I feel a great sense of accomplishment when he shuts off his phone and stuffs it into his pocket. I smile, celebrating that *the girls* have still got it. Not bad for ***cough*** thirty ***cough*** eight.

I sit across from him, pleased that he takes another long appreciative look when I gracefully cross my legs.

"How was your day?" I ask, smiling.

"Not bad. The kids are preparing for exams right now."

"I was going to ask you how you're able to send me messages during the day."

He smiles. "It's perfectly fine. It's a grade eight classroom. I write what they need to do on the board, and then I have time to read my messages while I'm at my desk."

I'm a little shocked since our exchange, at times, is *very* naughty. "They don't ever come to your desk and see what you're doing?"

"I'm careful to keep my phone down so it can't be seen."

"I'd be terrified of getting caught."

He shrugs and a sly grin forms across his lips as he leans closer and asks quietly, "Is your pussy shaved clean for Daddy?"

My face turns a shade of crimson and a look of satisfaction settles on his face. "Is it?" he persists.

"Yes," I finally manage to say, although I'm certain it's barely audible.

"So how do you think things are going? Do you think we're a good match?" He lifts his coffee to his mouth and stares at me over the rim of the mug.

"I think so." A wave of vulnerability washes over me. I force myself not to turn away. "I'm looking forward to getting to know you better," I add.

"I'm looking forward to fucking you." He leans in for privacy. "But you can't tell anybody, Daddy can get into trouble."

My heart starts to pound. I'm not opposed to trying new things, but I never expected that type of role-playing would make my panties wet. It's more likely because I'm extremely horny and there's a smoking hot man whispering dirty, nasty things into my ear.

He stands abruptly and it startles me.

"I have to go, it's getting late."

"I've only been here for half an hour."

Pulling on the back of my chair, he prompts me to get up and follow him to the door. I stall as he walks me to my car. He gives me a boyish grin as he steps forward, bringing that rock-hard chest closer. The anticipation makes my breath hitch as he slowly lowers his mouth and brushes his lips against mine. A shiver runs through my body, but I'm certain that it's just the cold Canadian winter air.

He pulls away. "I should get going before the roads get bad. I hear there's a storm moving in."

I nod in agreement, "If things work out between us, you can always stay at my place if the roads get bad."

Henry says nothing so I break the awkward moment of silence between us. "I was wondering if we could do a real date. Dinner and a movie?"

He zips up his jacket, then reaches into his pocket for his car keys. "I'm pretty busy this week."

"Can I have another kiss?" I blurt out desperately as I make a move toward him. I need one more before he goes. His lips are cold at first, making me more determined to heat things up. Grabbing his jacket, I pull him closer for a more passionate kiss.

His hands slide inside my open jacket to hold my waist and squeeze firmly. As I part my lips, deepening the kiss, he steps back, pulling away.

"I need to go."

"Are you sure? You could hang out a little longer. I'll make it worth your while." I blink my eyes and pause, shocked that I just said that out loud. Could I have sounded any more desperate? He stares at me with an amused grin.

"Let's do dinner and a movie next week."

"I'd like that." I bite my lip, resisting temptation. He's so damn hot and I'm eager to move forward. It's been ten years, and I think I'm finally ready for a monogamous relationship.

He walks toward his car without saying goodbye.

I stare, not sure what I'm waiting for. Suddenly, as if he can read my mind he turns and stares. "Be a good girl and Daddy will take care of you next week."

Chapter Two

Exhausted, I lock the door and drop everything on the floor in the hallway. It can stay there until later. Right now, I need to take off these shoes. At the end of the day, I'm not sure what possessed me to wear them to work. Who knew something so pretty could be so painful?

My eyes follow a long trail of discarded clothing that begins with a pair of sneakers and progresses along the way to the main floor bathroom. Outside the closed door, the last remaining piece of clothing sits, as it always does, as if my oldest son, Tanner, has magically disappeared, causing his jeans to slide to the ground.

I raise my voice slightly as I walk past the door. "Don't forget to spray this time."

I shake my head at his barely audible grumbling. "And turn the fan on."

The sound of rushed footsteps down the second-floor hallway warns that I best get out of the way in a hurry. "Whoa!"

"Hey, Mom!" My sixteen-year-old son, Dallas, bounds down the stairs and rushes past me.

"Hey! Where are you off to?" I wince at the sound of the slamming door. Applause and whistles erupt from the bedroom at the top of the stairs, followed by cursing. I knock once and then open the door, making a face at the smell of the day-old pizza sitting on the dresser. I wait for a break in the FIFA action and the current online conversation, with whomever he's playing with today. "Carson," I interrupt impatiently.

He gives me an annoyed look. "I'm busy."

I furrow my brow. "You're going to have lots of free time on your hands if I take away your PlayStation, so I'd lose the attitude."

He drops the controller in his lap and gives me a look. "What do you want?"

Gah. I shake my head. Once, just once, I'd like to come home and not have to deal with all the nonsense. Is that too much to ask? I fantasize about coming home at the end of a long workday to find the house clean, dinner made, and all three boys, showered and looking presentable. That's never going to happen.

"There's leftovers in the fridge. I'm going to meet Jen for dinner."

"You mean drinks." He picks up his controller and goes back to his game.

"Yes, I'll probably have a few of those, as well. I've earned them. It's been a hell of a week." I abandon the conversation, knowing that he really doesn't care how my week has been. He's already forgotten that I'm in the room.

I used to spend more time with my friend, Jen. Raising three boys on my own made it difficult both timewise and financially, so those times eventually faded away. Like my sex life and my sanity, as well as the ability to squeeze my ass into a size ten anything. Tonight, I'm looking forward to a few drinks and some girl talk. There's far too much testosterone in this house.

My phone lights up like a Christmas tree with all the notifications from lonely guys looking for someone to talk to tonight. While I try to run a brush through the curls in my hair, I receive a request for an online chat. Curiosity gets the best of me, so I clip my hair up on top of my head and accept.

MustangPete1975: Hello
Ladygwenevere: Hi
MustangPete1975: How are you this evening?
Ladygwenevere: I'm good. How about yourself?
MustangPete1975: I'm ok. So do you have a webcam?
Ladygwenevere: You know what. I'm just going out.
MustangPete1975: Stay home and talk to me. What are you wearing? Do you want to share pics?
Ladygwenevere: Sorry. I'm sure you'll find someone to keep you company. I'm not the girl for you.

I should have known better. I close the chat window and block MustangPete1975. I can't believe the nerve of some guys. It clearly says in my profile that I'm not looking for playtime. Nor am I looking for casual dating or hookups. That doesn't seem to stop them from messaging me looking for a little dirty talk, so they've got something to jack off to. I'm too old for that game. I want to find someone to share my life with. Not an easy task when I've kept myself well guarded over the past ten years. Everybody leaves me eventually, for one reason or another. It's hard to trust.

♥

"Booze! Quick!" I hang my purse over the back of the barstool and wiggle my short ass up onto the seat. "You pick these seats just because you like watching me get up here, don't you?"

Jen slides a drink over in front of me and grins. "Yes, it amuses me."

"I need new friends," I grumble.

"Yes, you do. All your friends are assholes."

"Agreed." I use the straw to stir my drink and then take a long sip. "Now that's a good mojito." My phone flashes and I open the dating app. "Oh look! There's a gentleman in Africa who would like to know if I'm looking for a husband."

"Really?"

"Yes! All I have to do is send him money to come to Canada." I raise my eyebrows as I continue to read, "Oh, wait. He wants money to bring his mother and three goats with him."

"Instant family. That's always awesome," Jen says sarcastically.

"Right? Just what I need. Three more *kids*."

Jen cringes. "So, tell me how things are going with the teacher."

I close the app on my phone. "Good. I think." The straw is slowing down my progress, so I abandon it and lift the glass to my mouth.

Jen grimaces. "I don't know how you can drink it like that without getting all that stuff in your mouth."

"Skill."

"And practice," she assumes.

Insert subject change here... "Can I ask you a question?"

"Of course."

"I like Henry. But..."

Jen narrows her eyes. "But?"

"Sometimes he seems to be interested in me, but other times he's not very attentive at all."

"Oh?" She waits for me to elaborate.

"It's odd. He seems distracted when he's with me, and I wonder if he's interested at all, then he comes out with something of an *amorous* nature and it surprises me."

"Amorous how?"

"Dirty."

"As in a sexual nature?"

"Yeah. And kinky." I'm familiar with the disapproving look on her face. "And to be honest, his kiss didn't really knock my socks off."

"Hmmm. Did he set up another date?"

"Sometime next week but he hasn't confirmed a day."

She drains her glass and uses her straw to separate the ice at the bottom. "What date will this be?"

"Four, I think."

She nods her head and sets her glass down on the table. "Well, I don't have a very good feeling about him." She motions to the bartender to bring another round.

"Isn't it a good thing to know that he's attracted to me and wants to have sex?"

Jen smiles. "Yes, I suppose so. It doesn't matter anyway." She hands the waitress a twenty-dollar bill as she slides our drinks across the bar.

"Why's that?" I ask.

"Because you've had three dates already."

"What does that mean?"

Jen snickers. "You have a three date expiry."

"A three date what?" I ask confused.

"Expiry." She lifts her glass to her mouth and takes a sip with a wry smile on her lips. "None of the men you've dated have ever made it to the fourth date."

My face turns red, and I'm not sure if its anger or the third mojito. "That's not true," I say defensively.

"Okay. Maybe three is wrong. Name one guy who made it past a fourth date," she demands.

My mind races through the names to prove her wrong, but I come up empty.

"Face it, sweetie. You're attracted to scumbags. If you don't have sex with them on the second date, you never hear from them again."

I blink, trying to comprehend her incredible nerve but the truth is, she's right. I've made a habit, lately, of dating men that I knew, deep down, would never be a good match for me.

"For the record," I protest. "I haven't had sex with every man I met, and I certainly don't have sex on the second date, with those I do."

Jen raises her eyebrows and I know she's made a good point. "Henry might be different," I say hopefully.

She gives me a sympathetic look. "It doesn't sound like it, I'm sorry to say."

To prove her wrong, I pick up my phone and shoot him a message.

Tori: Hi! I was wondering if you'd like to go out for dinner and a movie tomorrow night?

Almost an hour goes by and he still hasn't responded. Jen leans over, looks at my phone, and gives me that *I told you so* look. I guess she's right. Disappointment starts to set in and I'm already considering giving the African gentleman a second look. How much trouble could goats be? My phone vibrates and it startles me.

Henry: Tomorrow would be good.
Tori: Are you okay with wings? There's a little restaurant in Orangeville, not far from my house. It's one of my favorite places.
Henry: That's fine.

I look up from my phone and smile.

"I'm happy for you honey," Jen says unconvincingly.

"But?"

"Is he the right guy for you? Nice guys don't dirty talk on the third date if they're interested in having a relationship."

I scowl at her and she holds up her hand in defeat.

"Okay, I'm sorry. It's just that," she pauses, "After your ex-asshole, I really want you to find someone who treats you well."

"Can we talk about something else?"

Jen nods. "Let's talk about the new book I'm reading. It's a panty wetter."

"Oh, Lord. I can't read any more of those. I'm going to explode if I don't have sex soon."

"Just promise me that you won't rush into that with Henry. If he's a nice guy, he'll wait."

"What if I don't want to wait?"

"The man didn't make your toes curl when he kissed you, and you're still considering having sex with him?

"Yes. Is that wrong?"

"Seriously?"

"What?"

She swishes the ice cubes around in her glass and gives me a serious look. "Okay, let me ask you this question. Have you ever had a relationship where you develop an emotional connection first, or do you always jump right into the physical sex, and then try to build a relationship afterward?"

I can't honestly answer that. Well, I can, but I don't want to. "Emotional connection? As in *feelings*?" I snicker.

Jen frowns at me. "I didn't think so. You should try it. Maybe if you can find someone that you have a connection with first, the sex might be better. And then..." she slurs. "maybe they won't expire." She gives me a wide smile, and despite being aggravated by her comment, I forgive her. She's the one friend who stuck with me through all the ugly.

I dial all three of my boys, one after the other, and not one of them picks up. "I guess I'm taking a cab," I grumble.

"Good plan. Promise me. Take things slow with Harry."

I roll my eyes. "Henry," I correct.

"Meh, it doesn't matter." She waves it off and sways slightly as she gets to her feet. "He's almost expired already."

"Stop it," I warn, not feeling amused.

"*Best before* the fourth date."

"You're not funny," I advise again.

I slide into the cab feeling a little bit of a buzz from that last mojito. As the cab driver takes the corners at a ridiculous speed, I think about the things Jen said. I'm pretty good at looking after everyone else in my life, but not so good at looking after myself. She's right. If Henry is the right guy, he'll slow things down and wait. I take out my phone.

Tori: What are you doing?
Henry: Thinking about you. How about you? Are you getting ready for me?
Tori: I can't wait to see you again.
Henry: Tomorrow I will see ALL of you.

I grind my teeth. Jen's comment really struck a nerve with me and I know that she's just looking out for me.

Tori: About that. I was thinking we should wait a little longer.
Henry: Oh? Any particular reason?
Tori: To be honest, rushing into sex hasn't really worked well for me in the past. I want more in a relationship.
Henry: I see.
Tori: Is that okay?
Henry: Certainly.
Tori: I'm glad to hear that.

Cautiously, I step over the several pairs of size twelve sneakers, just inside the door. Apparently, the boys have friends over. That explains why nobody answered my calls. I ignore the frat boy cursing, coming from the basement, and go straight to my bedroom. Strange how long this hallway seems after a few drinks.

Pleased that I make it without incident, I crawl into bed and wait for Henry to reply to my last message. I try hard to steer the conversation in a nonsexual direction, but it's not easy. I'm restless and the booze didn't help matters. Why, oh why, did I let Jen get to me? After a few moments of polite banter, there are delays in Henry's messages, and it's not long before they fall off altogether. I stare at the ceiling, thinking about him. Waiting is the right thing to do. Now, all we have to do is work on that kiss.

Chapter Three

Once I finally got to sleep, I slept like a rock. I don't think I moved once in the night. My stomach protests loudly, waking me up. On my way down to the kitchen, I stop on the landing, blinking my eyes to make sure I'm not seeing things. I'm sure there's a perfectly reasonable explanation for the teenage boy sleeping on a mattress, in the middle of the family room floor, with a bucket beside him.

As I reach the bottom of the stairs, I notice the poor kid is shivering. I grab the throw blanket from the couch and begin to spread it out on top of him when he stretches, bringing into view the fresh plaster cast on his wrist and hospital bracelet.

That's a concerning discovery. I hope that someone let his parents know that he was safe for the night. Well, he was safe once he got here, but I'm not sure what happened prior to his arrival, and I can't wait to hear the story. He groans, seemingly in pain, as he rolls to his side and wraps himself in the blanket. Maybe I don't want to know what happened. If there was mischief afoot it seems probable that one, or all of my kids, were also involved.

I look at the kitchen, only a few feet away from where he's sleeping. I should carry on with my plans, eat some breakfast, and tidy up around here, making as much noise as possible. Instead, I put the Tylenol and a bottle of water on the floor beside him, and then put on my coat.

♥

When I arrive home from running a few errands in town, the mattress, and its habitant has magically disappeared. I drag the heavy bags of groceries into the kitchen. Establishing eye contact with Tanner, I grunt, as I drop them on the floor. "It would have been great if you offered to help."

"I'm busy," he mumbles with a mouth full of cereal.

"I can tell. Is that my salad bowl?"

Tanner shrugs.

"You're eating cereal out of the salad bowl?" I pick up the box he discarded on the counter and look inside. "Tanner! I just bought this cereal, and you've eaten the entire box in one serving?"

"I'm hungry."

"Oh well, that makes it okay then," I say sarcastically, as I collapse the box and fold it. "The money tree is bare," I growl as I stuff it inside the recycle bin. "I expected that cereal to feed the three of you for breakfast for at least a few days." I clench my teeth making my jaw ache, but as per usual, he's oblivious to my anxiety. "Do I want to know what happened to the boy that I found sleeping on the floor this morning?"

"Nope." He drops the spoon on the counter and without establishing eye contact, he tips the bowl to his mouth, chugging down the remaining milk.

I take a calming breath, but it doesn't help. "Do I *need* to know what happened? Tell me that you and your brothers didn't get into any trouble last night."

He drops the salad bowl into the sink and burps. "Calm your tits, woman."

I see a flash of red. "Excuse me? Have you forgotten that I'm your *mother*? There will be no calming of anything, least of all my tits, until I know that my children haven't been involved in anything illegal!"

He rolls his eyes and leans back against the counter. "Relax, Mom. He's a friend of Dallas'. They had a few beers at a party last night and he got into a little...disagreement...with someone's face."

"Everyone was here when I got home last night."

"Apparently they went out after that."

"Without letting me know? Wait...a few beers? Dallas was drinking?"

"Eddie is nineteen."

"Who the hell is Eddie?" I growl, on the edge of completely losing it.

"The guy with the cast."

"And he's hanging around with sixteen-year-olds? You're killing me, Tanner. Please tell me he wasn't drinking and driving with your brother in the car."

"He wasn't." He wipes his mouth on his sleeve. "Carson called me, and I picked them up from the hospital and brought them all here."

I gasp audibly. "Carson was there, too? You should have told me!"

"Yes, and he may, or may not, have driven them to the hospital. You were asleep so I left a note." He points at a piece of toilet paper on the counter with illegible scribbling on it. "Are we done here? I have to meet Ron at the auto parts store."

I lean against the counter and hold my head, trying to stop it from spinning. "Yes. Go."

He hesitates and then begins to walk away. "Don't worry, Mom. I looked after it."

"Tanner."

He turns and pauses, and at that moment, he's the spitting image of his father. The image momentarily stalls my thoughts. "It's not your responsibility to keep your brothers safe. It's mine. But thank you, for looking after it, Son. You're a good man."

He nods. "Not like Dad," he adds before turning to leave.

It breaks my heart. I often wonder what our lives would be like if I hadn't left. Maybe I should have just sucked it up, kept my mouth shut, and put up with the constant verbal abuse for the sake of the family. Would we be better off today? I'll never know the answer to that question. At times, it feels like I made a very selfish decision. My ex-husband was a very difficult man to live with, but boys need their fathers. I still have no idea what I did to turn his loving into loathing, or even *when* it happened. I'm even more confused as to why he was so angry when I left. It seemed to me that he wanted me to leave. Why else would he have made things unbearable for me?

I pull myself out of my own head and start getting ready for tonight. It's been ten years since I left Jim, and I need to put it behind me and concentrate on new relationships. I spend hours primping and preening for Henry tonight. I even shave my legs above the knee, just in case I have a momentary lapse of judgment. It's probably a wasted effort, since I have every intention of following Jen's advice. I'm positive that Henry isn't going to *expire*, but I'm going to do it just to prove a point.

I wonder if I can get away with wearing stockings. I pull the curtain to the side and shiver. Judging from the snow squalls, I should probably be wearing tights...or long johns. Somehow, I know that *Daddy* wouldn't approve.

My peaceful afternoon is suddenly disrupted by the sound of gunfire. The feeling that I'm now a prisoner of war means that Carson is finally awake and back online. Must be nice to sleep away the day. I'm shocked when I tip my phone to glance at the time and it's already 4:30 in the afternoon.

I knock on his door and open it without waiting for him to answer. "I'm going out tonight. The weather doesn't look too great, so I'd prefer you all stayed put. But if you decide to go out, please text me and let me know where you're going to be."

He ignores me and I try not to let it get me riled up, so it ruins my night. "And I don't care how good of an idea it seems at the time, you're not to get behind the wheel of anybody's car, for any reason." I wait for a reaction, but he continues to focus on taking out terrorists. "CARSON!"

He glances at me quickly through his peripheral vision. "Whatever."

"Good. I'm glad you understand because if there were ever to be a repeat of last night, you would most certainly lose your PlayStation and then you'd have to talk to *real* people." I pull the door closed with a little more passion then I was expecting and stand in the hallway. Now I know where they learned to slam doors.

I check for messages from Henry but there are none. Scrolling back through our messages I look for what time we agreed to meet, but it doesn't look like we decided on one.

Tori: Hey! What time would you like to meet for dinner tonight? I can't wait to see you again.

The longer I wait for a reply, the more time I have to second-guess my wardrobe decisions. After changing for the third time, I try phoning him but still get no response. I'll just head over to the restaurant and wait.

It's only a block and a half from my house to where we're meeting for dinner in the west end of town, but I drive. It's cold and slushy, and I'm not prepared to risk ruining hours of beautification due to frostbite and a case of hat head.

Anna, the beautiful raven-haired waitress greets me with a warm smile. "Sit anywhere you'd like," she offers as she hurries off into the kitchen. "I'll be with you in a minute."

A quick glance around the room confirms that Henry isn't there. I take off my coat and make myself comfortable at a table in the corner that will give us a little privacy on this busy Saturday night. I watch my phone as if I'm waiting for a ransom call.

The mobile app for the dating site flashes a message notification across the screen.

Papasmurf69: Hi. Do you like big cocks?

I growl out loud. Are you kidding me?

Ladygwenevere: Yes, Yes I do. Though I highly doubt yours is big enough or you wouldn't be single and looking for someone to talk to on a Saturday night.

Block. Block. Block.

Looking over the crowd, I wave to get the waitress' attention.

"Sorry about that." She puts a Jameson and ginger ale down in front of me. "It's crazy in here tonight."

"Is it sad that you know what I drink?"

"Well, it's one or the other." Her emerald green eyes sparkle as she looks over my outfit, from shoulder to shoes. "It doesn't look like it's a mojito kind of night."

I blush. "No, it's not."

She grins. "Nice! Who's the lucky guy?"

"The teacher I was telling you about."

"Oh, wow."

I'm intrigued by the look on her face. "What?"

"That's awesome! I didn't think he'd still be around."

I see the evidence of her Irish heritage as she pushes up her sleeves, revealing her Celtic tattoo. "Not you too," I groan. I lose her attention to a bunch of rowdy men, looking for another round of beer.

"Sorry," she says as she gets out her notepad. "I'll check on you in a bit."

I watch as she handles the group with patience and finesse that I'll never possess. I'm guessing she's used to dealing with their demands or she wouldn't last long in this business. I hope they tip her well for putting up with their bullshit, but I doubt it. They don't look like the generous tipping type.

It was late when I left the restaurant alone. I lost track of how many hockey games I watched, while keeping one eye on the door. I tried to convince myself he must have forgotten, but by ten p.m. I was officially worried. The snow squalls would have seriously impaired his visibility on the unpaved country roads he has to take into town.

I would have had a better sleep if he had acknowledged any of my messages, reassuring me he was safe. Still in my pajamas, I stumble down the stairs. I stop mid-way and feel thankful that there are no surprise guests on the living room floor. After checking my phone, I grab the stack of mail off of the counter and flip through it. The school logo catches my attention. Reluctantly I open it and begin to read.

"Carson!" I scream, making my way up the stairs. I knock once, then throw open the door. My anger turns to concern as I look around the room and find him missing. Moving to the next doorway, I open it and turn on the light. "Dallas?"

Startled he sits up and squints. "Mom! What the hell?"

"Do you know where Carson is?"

"In his room."

"No, he's not."

"What day is it?"

"Sunday."

He grunts and lays back down, pulling the blankets over his head. "He's at basketball."

I close my eyes, feeling ashamed. "I forgot, again. Damn it. I'm sure as hell not going to win mother of the year."

"I'll vote for you, if you let me go back to sleep," he grumbles from under the blanket.

I turn off the light and close the door. If I hurry, I can pick Carson up. I'm putting on my shoes when the door opens, and he walks in. He doesn't say a word and it makes me feel even worse. "Carson, I'm sorry."

He shrugs.

"Why didn't you wake me up?"

"You got home late and I didn't want to bother you."

"It's no bother. It's cold out there. I would have driven you. You're more important to me than sleep."

"Kevin's dad picked me up." He kicks off his shoes and starts upstairs.

"I got a letter from the school." He stops but doesn't look at me. "They want me to go in and speak to your marketing teacher. Is there a problem?"

"No. Everything's good." He begins to climb the stairs again. "Did it ever occur to you that maybe they want to tell you how great I'm doing?"

Immediately the guilt hits me hard in the chest. "I'm sorry," I holler after him, "I'll remember basketball next week," I promise.

"Don't worry about it. I'll walk."

The slamming door makes me jump. Within seconds, I hear the familiar, muffled whistles of FIFA 2017.

I busy myself most of the afternoon with chores around the house. Jen sends me accident listings she finds on the local social media and online news reports for last night. It's her way of being *helpful*. Is it wrong I hope she finds something?

All day long, I've had a bad feeling and it's not because I think he's been hurt in an accident. I've been here several times before. This is the reason I keep myself closed off, and never really let anyone in.

After several minutes of fidgeting, and trying to get comfortable, I still can't get into the movie I'm trying to watch on Netflix. I look over at the blank message screen on my phone and sigh. Finally, the curiosity gets the better of me and I log into the dating site.

I can't believe my luck! (Insert sarcasm here.) I have a message from a man without any teeth, who wants to know if I have medical and dental benefits. Hmmm, I'll pass. I scroll quickly through the next several messages, convinced English isn't their first language. Or second or third.

I'd like to say I'm stunned when Henry comes online, but I'm not. The stats down the side of the screen show he was actively online last night as well.

I sit completely still, trying to process what's just gone down. I can't believe it's true. Not this time. I open a chat window and send him a message.

Ladygwenevere: Hey! I'm glad to see that you're safe. I was worried. Did you forget that we had a date last night?

I watch as the message status indicates that he's read it and then I wait for a reply that never comes. I think I knew it wouldn't. After our last conversation, I felt something shift; I just didn't want to admit it. Apparently, he really wasn't okay with waiting for sex and building a relationship. I was hoping that Jen was wrong. I power off the TV and dump a full cup of tea down the drain. I don't need a man. I don't *need* anyone.

Going to bed early seemed like a good idea, but I lay there forever. The excruciating pain in my leg is a reminder of my ex-husband, Jim. Every time I close my eyes, his words echo in my mind repeatedly... *"Who would want you?"* For ten years that statement has haunted me, despite how hard I try to put it out of my mind. Maybe that's the reason I've chosen to be alone all these years. I thought I could finally move on and find someone to share my life with it, but it's painfully clear that Jim was right. This is where being emotionally numb has its benefits. Feelings make you weak and I'm a survivor. I always survive...I have no other choice.

My mind races, making me so edgy that it's impossible to relax. I run through an exercise my friend, Tanya, has given me to help me focus my thoughts and fall asleep. By the time I get to the part where I need to recite 'one thing I can see, one thing I can hear and one thing I can feel,' the silence comforts me, and the darkness hides my tears.

Chapter Four

Thinking about it all the way to the office the next morning, I work myself into a right foul mood. I sit in our morning meeting, still preoccupied with my thoughts, while the management team discusses the daily action plan. As usual, everyone is preoccupied with their phones. I scroll through my inbox, still looking for a reply from Henry. My boss mentions my name and I look up, completely lost to the conversation in the room. I take his annoyed expression as my cue to pay attention.

When I get back to my office, I try desperately to concentrate on my action items from the meeting. Instead, I find myself staring out my office window, watching the midday traffic and thinking about what happened. Jen is right, eventually, they all *expire*, and 'I' seem to be the reason.

Maybe I'm trying too hard. Maybe I should stop trying altogether. My frustration turns to anger. I'm done. I can't do this anymore. I'm not going to sit around crying and waiting for Mr. Wrong. The sooner I accept nobody wants me, the sooner I can put it behind me and focus on enjoying my life, alone. I don't need a partner to make my life fulfilling. People will only disappoint me and let me down. My life is a testament to that.

I log into my dating profile and scroll through the instructions on how to delete my account, ignoring the flurry of messages that start to push through from the men who've noticed me online. I can't wait for this to be over.

♥

For the next few days, I busy myself with work, shocked with the number of times I find myself tempted to go back online and reactivate my profile. Then I think about Henry, and I'm cured of my asshole obsession...for a few more hours, anyway. I have more than enough stress in my life right now.

My shoulders tense at a ruckus downstairs. I tip my glasses to the top of my head and wait it out, until the cursing starts to escalate, and the traditional slamming of doors begins.

"What's up?" I ask Tanner as I reach the foyer.

"My car wouldn't start again," he snaps. "I need to figure out what's wrong with it."

"Did you replace the battery?"

"It's not the battery," he answers, annoyed.

He rummages through his toolbox looking for something in particular.

"Do you need a boost?"

"NO!" He throws wrenches and screwdrivers aside.

It's not like Tanner to have a meltdown. Something else is going on. "You can borrow my car until you get it fixed," I offer, wanting to help.

"I don't want to borrow your car. I want to fix mine! I can't figure it out because I'm fucking stupid," he says, sounding defeated.

"Tanner..." I say sympathetically. "You're way too hard on yourself."

"Stop, Mom." He tries to hide the emotion in his voice. "I miss Grampa," he says, avoiding eye contact with me. "He would know what to do."

"Yeah, he would." Now I understand. He steps back as I reach out to give him a consoling hug, and I try not to feel hurt. "Every car we ever owned was a reject of some sort. Grampa always knew how to keep them running."

None of us were prepared for my dad to leave us so soon. Least of all, Tanner. They were very close. I try to give him an encouraging smile. "Hey, listen. You're a smart boy. Just like your Grampa. I have no doubt that you'll figure it out."

He looks at me as if there's something he'd like to say but remains silent as he turns to leave.

"Let me know how I can help," I finally add, wondering if there will ever be a conversation in this house that doesn't end with a slamming door when I'm mid-sentence.

I try to finish the report I was working on, but I can't stop thinking about my dad. I don't allow myself to miss him. It's how I deal with it. He was the glue that helped keep my family together when my life went to hell. He stayed with the boys when I had to work late, helped them with science projects, and attended every sporting event.

An incoming message interrupts my thoughts. Just in time, since I seem to be on the verge of an emotional breakdown. Heaven forbid I allow myself to cry. Sad is a *feeling* after all, and I don't do those.

Unknown Number: Hi.

It's probably another one of my friends or family who's bought a new phone and is trying to reestablish their contact list.

Tori: Hi. Who is this?

Unknown Number: I was away on a trip for a friend's birthday.

I stare at the screen, trying to make sense of it.

Tori: Sounds like fun but who is this?
Unknown Number: It's Roger.

That's kind of mysterious. I don't know anyone named Roger.

Tori: Roger who?
Unknown Number: From online dating.
Tori: ??
Unknown Number: JohnDeere1978.

Now, I have an interesting situation. I think I remember this man, and he had a kind smile. It's been weeks since I gave him my cell number. I hadn't given up on him, I had completely forgotten about him altogether. I assign his number in my contacts.

Tori: I decided to take a break from the online dating thing.
Roger: Sorry, Gwen. I was on a boat. I'm back now.
Tori: I'm not really looking for anyone.

Wait...Gwen? Who the hell is Gwen? I shake my head. Just another guy who cares so little about details that he can't even bother to get my name right.

Roger: I'm not a knight. Just a guy.

What? I laugh out loud when I figure out what he's talking about.

Tori: My name is Victoria. You can call me Tori. Gwenevere was just my profile name.
Roger: Oh, Sorry. Can I call you? I'm not good at this texting thing.

This is probably a bad idea, but the boys are driving me crazy and Jen is on a trip to Quebec City. I really need to have an adult conversation. This time, I'll make sure I don't get all caught up in the romance of it. There's never going to be a fairytale ending for me. When my phone rings a moment later, I become nervous and freeze up. It rings three or four times before I finally answer. You'd think I'd be used to this part by now.

"Hey," I say, trying to hide my sudden onset of angst.

"Hey, I thought maybe you changed your mind. I almost hung up."

"Sorry."

"It's okay," he assures me. "I'm a little nervous too."

"I was surprised to get your message."

"Yeah, well, I'm sorry it took so long. It was my buddy's birthday and we went away for a few days."

"Oh. That sounds like fun."

"I'm not going to lie. This online dating thing is way out of my comfort zone. It took him all week to convince me to call you."

I let out a small laugh. "I know what you mean."

He coughs a few times and then clears his throat. "Sorry about that, I think I'm getting a cold."

"No doubt, if you were out on a boat in the middle of January."

"A boat?"

I scroll back through the text messages. "Yes, you said you were on a boat."

He laughs, "No, I was on a trip, not on a boat. I told you I was bad at texting."

"Oh, that's funny. Have you had any luck on that site?"

"Only bad luck. How about you?"

"The same. That's why I recently decided to delete my account."

"That's a shame. Were you a member for a long time?"

"It seems like forever. What about you?"

"I've only been on there about six months."

"Oh." *Rookie*, I think to myself. "How long have you been single, if you don't mind me asking? I'm afraid I can't see your profile anymore since I closed my account."

"I've been single for about a year."

Oh boy, there's a red flag. I immediately start to feel apprehensive. "Are you sure you're ready for dating?"

He apologizes after another short coughing spell. "You're not the first person to ask me that. I think so. Is there any way to know for sure until you actually try to *move on?*"

"Good point." I'm starting to feel a little more at ease.

"I know I won't be a good match for some, but I figured I'd start with looking for a companion with similar interests to spend time with. That's a good base to start building a relationship on, I think."

I begin to question his intentions. I'm not looking for an activity buddy or a friend with benefits. "Are you looking for a long-term relationship?"

"For sure. I'm not the kind of guy who serial dates women. I'm not looking for a one-night stand or an occasional fling."

There's something soothing about the sound of his voice. His deep, gruff-sounding tone has erased my anxiety.

"I'm not looking to propose on the first date," he chuckles. "But I think spending time with someone and getting to know them is important. You have to have at least some similar interests and likes. I think the best relationships are ones that are born on a solid foundation of respect and friendship then blossom into more."

I'm officially impressed. And completely skeptical. "I agree."

"Good. I'd like to get to know you better. Would you meet me for dinner on Saturday?"

I know my schedule is clear, but I still hesitate.

"I'm in Brampton. Where do you live?" he asks, clearing his throat.

"I live in Orangeville."

"So, is that a yes?"

"We can meet halfway, if you like. Or I can drive to Brampton." I have no idea why I'm doing this.

"That doesn't feel right. I should be coming to you."

"I don't mind. Really," I assure him. At least this way I can leave when I want. "There isn't anything halfway between us, but farmland and I drive to Brampton all the time."

"I guess that would be okay. I'll meet you at Montana's in Brampton on Saturday."

♥

Social media and cell technology are comfortable skills for me. My cell phone is seldom more than a few feet away, if not in my hand. I continually check and check again, waiting for messages from Roger. It's an all too familiar situation and it makes me regret my decision. I should have stuck to my guns and called it quits on this dating thing. I've spent plenty of time alone over the years and I didn't die. I hate this feeling of desperation. Loneliness. Feelings that are quickly forgotten when a message notification flashes across my screen.

Roger: Do you like camping?

Okay, so that's a little random. I haven't heard from him in two days and that's what he leads with? I shrug. I'm just glad to hear from him.

Tori: I do. I like camping and outdoor stuff. But I also like doing things that allow me to get all dressed up pretty.
Roger: That's good to know. I have no objection to putting on a fork and a tie once in a while.

I scratch my head...ummm...A what?

Roger: Suit and tie. Stupid autocorrect.
Tori: Ah. I wondered. lol Do you know what comes after forking?
Roger: What?
Tori: Spooning.

I laugh out loud at my own joke. It's a classic.

Roger: I have a wolf picture in my bedroom.

What the? This is just getting more awkward. Not sure how to respond, I put my phone down on the counter while I make myself a cup of tea. Before I can even put the milk away, he's calling.

"Hey. Sorry I was just making a tea."

"I thought I'd call. Obviously, I wasn't joking about how bad I am at texting."

I'm concerned by the hoarse sound of his voice. "Are you feeling alright?"

"Not really. I caught something when I was away. After I talked to you the other night, I couldn't breathe. I went to the doctor yesterday. He gave me antibiotics and told me to take some time off work."

"Oh, no, I'm sorry. I guess we should postpone our dinner."

"You don't mind?" he asks, surprised.

"Of course not, if you're not feeling well." Something tells me that he's looking for an out. But that's just me. Always waiting to be disappointed. Usually, I'm right on the money.

"The doc says I'm not contagious, but you never know. It's up to you. I still want to meet you."

He wheezes and it concerns me. Maybe he's telling the truth, but I need to do the right thing here. "We can postpone dinner until you're better. You should stay home and take care of yourself."

"I'm trying. My friend Linda brought me over some turkey soup."

"Oh." I unsuccessfully hide the uncomfortable tone in my voice.

"My buddy's wife," he offers.

Now I feel awkward. What was that all about? I haven't even met the man yet and I had a momentary bout of jealousy? I know I need to get my shit under control and not get emotionally attached to this man. This is going to be nothing but a few days of companionship then he'll move on. "I'm sorry. You don't owe me an explanation."

"I'm not trying to get out of dinner."

I try to deny that's what I was thinking, but it doesn't work. After several minutes of us both trying to do the *right* thing we've yet to come to an agreement and it's exhausting.

He coughs several times, and then ends it in a raspy voice, "Okay. I'm putting my foot down and making a decision. We're going to meet on Saturday like we originally planned."

Now that's enticing. I like a man who can take charge. Don't get me wrong; I'm not a weak woman or a pushover. I've had to make *all* the decisions for the past ten years and meeting a man, who can take on that responsibility when I need him to, is kind of sexy.

Chapter Five

Roger didn't exaggerate about his inadequacy with texting. Every day he sends me a message and it's painful. Today is finally Saturday and he assures me that he's feeling better and looking forward to meeting me for dinner. I'd be lying if I said I wasn't still worried and it's not about catching something.

Am I crazy? I wonder about that the entire drive into Brampton. I'm used to driving in the snow, so that's not what has me questioning my sanity. I've done this first date thing so many times over the past few months, that I'm an old pro at it. We'll meet, eat dinner, and I'll be home by 9:30.

I pull into the parking lot and get out my phone. I'm early so I'll send him a quick text.

Tori: Hi. I'm here early. I'll wait for you inside.
Roger: I'm here too. I'm waiting just outside the front door.

Impressive. As I take slow careful steps on the snow in my heels, I can see a man standing on the curb at the end of the dimly lit parking lot. It's been a few weeks since I deleted my account and I wish I could remember better what he looked like. I purposely didn't ask him to exchange pictures during any of our recent exchanges, since that request, with other men, has gone all sorts of wrong.

From a distance, I notice the few days' growth of meticulously manicured stubble that frames his face and chiseled jawline. His broad shoulders taper down to a reasonably well-toned body. I take a sharp breath, filling my lungs with cold air. I try to prevent myself from feeling hopeful, but this man is very sexy. Not to mention he smells delicious from a few feet away. I'm still not entirely sure that it's him, until he steps down into the light.

"Victoria?" He smiles and offers me a hug.

"It's really great to finally meet you." I'm not sure if he's nervous or if it's the cold Canadian air that makes him shiver slightly.

"Here," he offers me his hand, "Let me help you inside. It's slippery in spots."

Safely inside the restaurant, the waitress shows us to our table. Roger helps me with my coat and waits for me to sit before he takes a place directly across from me. The restaurant is busy, and, at times, I struggle to hear him over the noise as we spend a few minutes refreshing our knowledge of each other. The *job interview* Jen calls it. The rundown of all the important stuff and the exchange of sexual history and health, be it ever so sad that it's a necessary safety measure. Society has evolved well past the model of saving yourself 'til marriage and death do you part.

It occurs to me that there's another important question that I haven't asked.

"Do you have any kids?" I ask curiously, "I don't recall if we ever discussed that."

"Yes, I have a daughter, Molly. She's seven. You?"

"Oh, well hopefully this isn't a deal-breaker, but I have three sons. They have a lot more mileage on them than that. Tanner is eighteen, Dallas is sixteen and Carson is fourteen."

"So you had the two-year plan."

I smile. "Yeah, something like that."

"I have full custody of my daughter. I hope that's not a deal-breaker for *you*."

It's not as common for fathers to have full custody and I wonder why, but it doesn't matter to me in the least. "No, it's not."

"Good. I'm lucky my mom and dad are around to help out. Mo is quite happy to spend time there if I need to do things." He folds his menu and places it in front of him, "Like going on a date with a beautiful woman."

I start to blush. "When does your ex take her?"

"She doesn't."

"Not at all?"

"Nope. I think I want fajitas. Have you decided?"

I start to get the feeling I've hit a nerve. I struggle to remember the details of his profile but I'm pretty sure he isn't a widower. How embarrassing would it be if I asked him now? "Fajitas sound great. I'll do the same."

Over the course of our meal, Roger ticks all the boxes on the 'gentleman' list and polite conversation requirements. He's even made me laugh a few times.

He wipes the remnants of his last fajita from his mouth and places his napkin on the table.

"Did you enjoy your dinner?" I ask.

"I did, but next time, remind me to order them without that horrible sauce."

I smile. He's planning for the *next time*. "I was just thinking the same thing. Who puts apple butter on fajitas?"

"Horrible."

"Agreed."

He reaches for the bill when the waitress brings it to the table.

"I can get that," I offer.

"Not a chance. I invited you out, so I'll pay."

"At least let me pay for my own," I protest.

Ignoring me, he places his credit card in the folder and hands it to her.

While we wait for her to complete the transaction, I sit back and take a really good look at him. We've been here for a few hours and not once have I regretted my decision or wished it was over. I've thoroughly enjoyed his company and the conversation. Before my brain can remind me of the most likely future outcome, the words are out of my mouth. "It's still kind of early," I mention casually.

He pauses, staring at me with those baby blue eyes. It makes me nervous because there's definitely chemistry between us.

"What are you thinking?"

"I dunno." I blush. "I'm just wondering if you wanted to hang out some more."

"That would be nice, but how about tomorrow instead?" He stands and puts his wallet back in his pocket.

I begin to feel very insecure. History always has a way of repeating itself and I was silly to think that might change now. "Oh, of course. I understand."

He looks at me with narrowed eyes. "Understand what?" Holding up my jacket, he waits for me to join him.

I get a tingly kind of feeling as he guides my coat over my shoulders and untucks my hair from the collar. The words stick in the back of my throat and come out all...pathetic sounding. "I understand if you don't want to hang out." When I turn, he's giving me a look I can't quite identify.

"Sorry, it's not that I don't want to spend more time with you, but...to be honest...these antibiotics are kicking my ass. I can barely keep my eyes open."

Now I feel really stupid. "Oh, Roger. I'm sorry. I've been enjoying your company so much that I've completely forgotten you're not feeling well."

"That, and it's getting late. You should be getting home."

"You know, I haven't even looked at my phone since I got here. I have no idea what time it is."

"It's after eleven p.m. I'll walk you to your car."

"That's really sweet of you."

"Well, I'd feel bad if you managed to kill yourself in those shoes."

I look down at my designer pumps and grin. "Duly noted. Next time I'll wear combat boots."

"Awesome, I dig a chick in camo," he teases, as he escorts me safely to the car. He waits outside the door with his hands in his pocket and jacket undone, standing guard. I roll down my window and give him a questioning look, but he doesn't respond. "What are you doing?" I finally ask.

"Waiting."

"For?"

"Just making sure you get on your way safely." He bends down and leans on the window, putting himself at my eye level. Suddenly, something on the dashboard catches his attention and he raises his eyebrows. "You're almost out of gas."

"Oh." I shrug it off. "I should be able to make it to Orangeville on a quarter of a tank."

"It's not a good idea to take a chance like that. What if you don't make it?"

"You're right, but I have an auto club membership." I love that he's genuinely concerned.

"There's a station on your way out of town." He digs his keys out of his pocket. "I'll follow you there."

I'm confused. "Why?"

"It's almost midnight. You're not driving home on less than a quarter tank, and I'm not letting you stop for gas in Brampton, alone."

"I'll be fine," I insist.

"Oh, I know you will. Because I'm going to follow you over there and make sure you are."

I'd argue, but it seems like there's no point. He's made up his mind and surprisingly, I'm okay with it.

I watch him walk to his car and I'm amused. Okay, so he drives a Volkswagen. I can overlook that, I think. He follows me out of the parking lot, but once we pull out onto the road, I turn up the music and I'm gone.

I'm waiting for a pump to become available when he arrives at the gas station a few minutes later. Who knew that a gas station would be this busy at midnight on a Saturday? He pulls in behind me and gets out of his car. The temperature has dropped several degrees, making me shiver, as I lift the nozzle off the cradle.

"It's cold. Go sit inside," he says, taking it out my hand.

"I'm not letting you stand out here in the cold and pump my gas."

"Yes, you are," he insists.

"You're sick!" I protest.

He locks his eyes to mine, and pauses a moment, considering his approach. "Exactly, I'm already sick. And you don't need to get sick. So..."

I surrender the handle but there's no chance that I'm going to sit in the car. There's something about him that makes me want to stay close to him.

I lean against the cold car and watch him pump gas. My mind races in thousands of directions all at once.

"Aren't you cold?" he asks, as he hangs up the nozzle.

"Freezing."

He gives me a half-smile as he opens the door. "Then get out of the cold."

I give up. He's determined to send me on my way tonight. "Okay. You win." I say, avoiding eye contact. "Thank you for dinner."

My heart pounds when he leans in closer to me. Raising his hand to my cheek, he holds it gently while he presses a tender kiss there. At least I think it's a kiss. It's such a gentle brush of his lips, I'm not really sure.

"Good night." He waits for me to climb in and buckle up. "Go straight home and message me when you get there."

Again, I think about protesting, but he closes the door. "Good night," I say through the closed window. I watch him through my rearview mirror, not entirely sure what I'm waiting for. I suppose I just don't want to go.

♥

I can't stop thinking about him, all the way home. The minute I walk through the door, I let him know that I've made it safely. He responds to my message with one word.

Roger: Thanks

I don't sleep well. I toss and turn and fidget all night long, fighting an internal struggle I'm not sure I want to lose. As soon as my eyes open in the morning, I roll to my side and grab my phone.

Tori: Hi. I was wondering if you would like to have a coffee with me today.

I climb out of bed and pull a sweatshirt over my head. I'm too tired to stop and put a bra on, but I don't want to traumatize my children. Hopefully, they'll all still be asleep. I'm halfway down the stairs when I smell Toaster Strudels. I place my hand on my forehead and squeeze my eyes closed. Carson.

"Hey, Buddy, give me two minutes to get dressed and I'll take you to basketball."

"It's okay, I don't need a ride."

I try not to show my disappointment. "Can I pick you up?" I watch as he wraps his Toaster Strudel in a piece of paper towel and stuffs it in his backpack. "Can I at least make you a better breakfast?"

"My ride's here." He grabs an apple off the table and takes a bite on his way out the door. "See? I'm eating healthy."

I watch out the kitchen window as he gets into an unfamiliar red car. My phone interrupts the guilty feelings.

Roger: Yes. Coffee. Tim Hortons in Erin. Do you know where it is? On the main road through town.
Tori: Yes, I know it. What time?"
Roger: In an hour. I have to shower first.
Tori: See you then.

♥

I pull into the parking lot ten minutes early, and he's already there. I'm struck by the smell of his cologne when he opens my door. Does anything smell better than a freshly showered man?

"You look pretty." He holds out his hand and helps me out of the car. All this attention is something new for me and I'm already blushing. He insists I find a place to sit while he gets our drinks. I stare as he stands in line, admiring how tempting the casual black jeans make his ass look.

He chats with everyone around him. He has one of those smiles that lights up a room and instantly makes those around him feel comfortable.

He returns with two teas and a sandwich and sits across from me. Unwrapping it, he offers me half. I haven't even thought about eating today, but now I'm starving.

"What is it?" I ask, while my stomach grumbles loudly.

"It's a turkey club with regular mustard. I don't like that honey mustard shit."

I look up, a little surprised.

"Oh, I did it again, didn't I?" he asks embarrassed.

"What?"

"I have a habit of saying the wrong things out loud. I'm sorry."

"It's all good."

"Sometimes my mouth opens, and I say stuff without thinking. I hope I don't ever offend you or hurt your feelings."

"I can't imagine you ever doing that on purpose."

"It happens a lot. I have no filter."

I take half the sandwich from his hand and take a bite.

"I'm not a fan of honey mustard either. Are you lonely way over there?"

He laughs once. "I like to be able to look at your face when I'm talking to you."

"I see. What would you like to talk about?"

He twists the plastic lid on his takeaway cup, making sure that the opening is not in line with the seam. I thought I was the only person who did that.

"We could talk about your driving."

"My driving?"

"Going a little fast last night, weren't you?"

"Oh, I'm sorry. Did your bunny have a hard time keeping up?" I tease.

"There was a cop on one of the side streets. You're lucky he didn't go after you."

"Very lucky," I acknowledge. "I like *fast*."

He nods his head, trying to hold back a grin. "I noticed."

I can tell he's biting his tongue and it amuses me. "So, refresh my memory." I wipe my mouth with my thumb since he didn't think to get napkins. "What kind of work do you do?"

"I work in a warehouse. Shipping and receiving."

I giggle as he bites his sandwich and a blob of mustard escapes out the bottom and lands on his shirt.

"You think that's funny, do you?" he asks, getting up to grab some napkins.

"I do," I snicker. "Usually it's me that wears my lunch. Have you always lived in Brampton?"

"No, only since I was eighteen."

"I was born in Toronto," I offer. "I grew up in Brampton. I moved to Orangeville after I was married. I was eight months pregnant when we moved. We couldn't afford a house in the neighborhood where I grew up." I stuff the last piece of sandwich in my mouth and wait. "Where did you live before Brampton?"

"You're not going to believe me."

"Try me."

"I grew up in Orangeville."

"No way!" Now that's funny. "Maybe we were like two ships that passed in the night."

He shrugs. "Maybe. You never know."

I excuse myself to use the restroom, and when I return to the table, I attempt to slide in beside him. He looks at me, somewhat confused.

"You don't mind, do you? These places are always so cold." It's hardly a subtle move, but my flirting up to then seems to be an epic fail. I try to ease my way closer to him, wanting to feel the warmth of his body. There's something about him that pulls me toward him and makes me crave his touch. I guess I'm one of those girls who fall *too quickly*. Yet another reason why I send men running for the hills.

"I should get going," he announces, as he crumples up the paper from his sandwich and gathers up the rest of the waste. "Mo was out shopping with my mother today. I have to pick her up soon."

"Oh, of course. I'm sorry."

"Sorry for what? Why are you always apologizing?"

"I'm sorry for keeping you from your daughter." I slide to the end of the booth and stand so he can get out.

"It's all good."

On the way back to the car, I edge my way closer to him. He glances at me from the side when our arms brush together.

When he opens my car door, I get that weird feeling again. I'm not sure if he's attracted to me or not.

"Tuesday is my birthday," he announces. "I was wondering if you'd let me pick you up at work and take you out for lunch?"

"Well, if it's your birthday, I think I should take you out for lunch."

"Deal. But I'll pay."

"Not a chance."

"I insist."

"You'll lose this argument." I toss my stuff into the car.

"Okay, we'll see," he says, sounding a little agitated. "It's a date."

It *is* a date. It will be our third date in four days, but something just doesn't seem right.

❤

Feeling like I need to talk things through; I do what every girl does. I call my best friend.

"So, let me get this straight. He opens your doors, helps you with your coat, and is a complete gentleman?" Jen clarifies.

"Yes."

"That bastard!" she says sarcastically.

"Stop it, I'm serious here. I think I like him."

"You like them all, at first."

I growl, "It's hard to explain. I'm attracted to him, but he doesn't seem to be interested in me."

"Why do you say that?"

"He sits on the opposite side of the table from me, and when we're walking, he leaves a lot of space between us."

"How many dates have you been on?"

"Two."

"Since Saturday?" she confirms, "Ah. I see the problem."

"What?"

"He's a nice guy."

"What does that mean?" I ask feeling annoyed.

"Honey, I love you. But you are the queen of self-sabotage. Things are looking good. You're two dates in, so you're preparing yourself..."

"Don't you dare say it," I warn.

"Have you ever dated a good man before?"

"I don't think I've ever met one before." I roll up the rim on my Tim Hortons coffee and frown at the *please play again* message printed there. "I never win on these."

"So what are you going to do?"

"I don't know. I'm still not convinced he's interested in a romantic relationship with me."

"I thought you said he kissed you?"

"It was a brief, polite peck goodbye on the cheek!"

"But it was still a kiss!" Jen curses under her breath. "It's only been three days!"

"How long do I wait? I was feeling a little playful last night, so I texted him a dirty picture from the Internet."

Jen groans, "Tell me you didn't."

"I did."

"And?" she asks frustrated.

"He sent me back a picture of two people cuddling, romantically."

"That's sweet. Seriously! What is your issue?"

"Shouldn't there be some excitement? I'm looking for sparkle and I'm getting fizzle."

"Poor guy is expiring as we speak." She picks up her jacket and deposits her empty cup in the trash on the way out the door. "Give the nice guy a chance. I'm rooting for the nice guy!"

Chapter Six

I step over several oily engine parts in the driveway. Following the trail into the house, I call out, "Tanner?"

"What?"

"Uhhh. What's going on?"

"I'm watching videos on how to replace the brakes on my car."

"That's kind of a big job, isn't it?"

He takes his eyes off the YouTube video on his phone for a brief moment. "Not really."

The overly cautious mother in me can't keep my mouth shut. "Is that safe?"

He doesn't say a word, but I can tell that I've struck a nerve.

"Tanner? Maybe brakes are something you should leave to someone who knows what they're doing."

He angrily shoulders past me. "Thanks for the vote of confidence, Mom."

As he closes the door behind him, without saying goodbye, I close my eyes and take a small breath, trying to relieve some of the tension. I rummage through the pantry. Maybe chocolate will help. Shamelessly, I open a package of chocolate chips and dump some in my hand.

"MOM!"

I jump, spilling them on the floor. "Dallas? What's wrong?"

"I need a ride to Eddie's."

"Now?" I look at my watch. "It's a school night."

"Yeah. My homework is done."

I grab my keys, deciding that it's a good time to discuss his new friend, Eddie. While I'm driving, he's captive to my lecture on what's acceptable behavior for a boy his age. I'm fairly sure that it goes in one ear and out the other, but at least I've had the conversation. That somewhat redeems my recent parenting fail, right?

I'm on my way home when I get a call from Carson. "Mom? Did you forget you were meeting with my teacher tonight?"

"Fuck." I'm out of the running for mother of the year *again*. I hang my head in shame. "No. No, I didn't forget. I'll be home to pick you up in two minutes. Wait outside."

♥

An hour later we arrive back home. "Well, that was interesting," I say, finally breaking the silence. "So much for them wanting to tell me how awesome you're doing." I toss my keys on the kitchen table. Carson wisely keeps his mouth shut. "Go upstairs." I clench my jaw so tightly it cracks. When I hear his bedroom door close, I move to the family room and plop myself down on the sofa in the dark. I lean back and stare at the ceiling, praying for strength. Some days it feels like it's too much.

I flip through a million choices on Netflix and can't find one single thing that interests me. The small table lamp in the corner illuminates a section of the bookshelf and it draws my attention, like a beacon lighting the way. I run my finger along the spines of the books, wondering if it's a coincidence or a message.

I choose one of the worn out, often read, Louis L'Amour paperbacks and settle on the couch. Folding back the cover, I smile as I trace my finger over my dad's signature on the cover page. He always signed them there, so he knew which books were his and which ones he borrowed from someone else. I flip through the yellowed, dog-eared pages and laugh once, remembering that he used to say that he marked the *good pages* for my mother to read. She didn't share his love for books or adventure, but he always hoped she'd have some interest in the dirty bits.

I pull the blanket over my legs and turn to the first page. I don't know how long I read for before I fell asleep on the couch. When I wake, in the middle of the night, I have a very strong feeling that my dad is with me, patiently waiting for me to turn to the next page. I know it's not possible, but as my eyes adjust to the darkness, I scan the room, looking for him. It's these moments, the quiet ones, where I allow myself to miss him. I'll never get my head around how someone you love so much can be there one day and gone the next. Maybe that's the reason I choose men I know will fail. I know they won't be sticking around and it's over before my heart can become the collateral damage. Clearly, endings are not something I do well. It's been almost ten years, and I've denied myself the right to mourn the death of my father or the end of my marriage.

I make my way through the dark house to my bedroom. One small tear is all I permit myself, as I crawl into bed. Tomorrow I have a lunch date with Roger, and I know what I have to do.

♥

As usual, Roger is early for our lunch date and waiting for me outside the restaurant. Before I can even put the car in park, he's at my door. Knowing that I'm about to end it makes me feel a little sad when I see him. My nerves grab a hold of me as he helps me out of the car and escorts me into the restaurant.

I follow the hostess to our table and try to gracefully slide over into the booth so he can join me. As usual, he sits on the opposite side. He's the poster child for polite, respectful guys. Funny, I always thought that would be a trait that a woman would look for in a man, but I wonder if there's such a thing as being *too gentlemanly*. Now I'm convinced that he's looking for an activity buddy. I'm making the right decision.

"So how's your birthday been so far?" Sitting across from him today has its perks. His eyes are the most brilliant blue. They sparkle when he smiles, and it somewhat settles my anxiety. I know at that moment that I'm in big trouble.

"Well, it was just another day until now. You look beautiful."

I blush. I'm definitely overdressed for a day at the office in my little black dress and brand new shoes. Despite mulling over our impending demise, I spent half an hour hiding in the office restroom primping for this lunch. Odd, since I spent the past twenty-four hours coming up with all the reasons why this relationship isn't going to work and preparing myself for the breakup. Maybe, deep down, I'm hoping I can inspire him to turn it up a notch today. I'm not sure what suddenly comes over me. "Do you like me?" I blurt out.

He narrows his eyes. "Of course I do."

"I mean, do you want to have a *romantic* relationship with me?"

"Excuse me?" he says, confused.

"I'm sorry," I say, rambling a mile a minute now that I'm on a roll. "It's just, you're always so far away from me, and so...nice."

"Nice is a bad thing?" He sits back and continues to listen.

"Do you like sex?"

He looks at me, shocked. "What?"

"Do you want to have sex with me?" I become flustered. "Not right now. I mean eventually." I stop myself and try to get my thoughts together. "I'm not really explaining myself very well. It's just that, I can't tell if you like me or not. It kind of feels like we're sliding into the friend zone."

I take a breath and wait through a very awkward pause. "So, do you?"

He scratches his head, still looking bewildered. "Yes."

Is he serious? Yes, what? "You're attracted to me?"

"Yes," he says calmly.

I can see his mind is racing but he says nothing.

"Good." I'm relieved. "I'm attracted to you. But, Roger, you need to turn it up a notch; show me your game. Give me something!"

He sits forward, folding his hands in front of him on the table and stares at me. The anticipation makes my heart start to pound. He nods. The glimmer in his eyes is so much more powerful than their usual baby blue.

Excusing myself from the table, I pretend to make a trip to the restroom and intercept the waitress for the bill. There's not a chance in the world I'm going to make him pay for lunch on his birthday.

The restaurant is buzzing with men talking about business, and on my way back to the table, I notice a man at the next table looking my way. He's definitely checking me out and appreciating what he sees. He smiles and says hello as I pass, and I politely smile back.

"So you paid the bill," Roger confirms, as I sit back down.

I grin, proud of myself. "Yes, I did. Happy birthday."

"Okay, you got me this time," he says, getting to his feet. The man at the next table is not subtle. He's still staring at me and Roger has taken notice. He holds up my jacket and guides it over my shoulders. Leaning into my ear, he whispers. "Did I mention that I'm half Irish and half Scottish?"

"No, I don't think so."

"Trust me, your friend over there doesn't want to see my temper."

When I turn, with wide eyes and raised eyebrows, he takes my hand, lifts it to his mouth and places a kiss on the back of it. "Thank you, for lunch."

"You're welcome. I'm sorry I have to leave so soon." I start toward the door and look down at my hand. Roger still has it firmly clasped in his and he's not letting go.

"Let's get you back to work." As we pass by the other table, his drawn out, icy glare at the man sitting there sends an unmistakable message. He says few words on the way to the car and that's okay with me. I'm somewhat amused by the small display of jealousy that just took place. I scan the parking lot for his car. "Where did you park?"

"I'm beside you."

We're only a few feet away from my well-loved 2003 Chrysler and I still don't see his ride. "Where?"

The edges of his lips start to curl into a mischievous grin. "Right there, beside you."

I look to the left, and I look to the right. Now I'm sure that he's messing with me. He erupts into a full smile that has him glowing, as he presses the remote starter in his hand, illuminating the lights.

I take a long appreciative look. Running my hand along the spoiler, I admire the sparkle of the metallic black paint in the sunlight. "You drive a brand new Camaro?"

His chest puffs out. "Not just a Camaro, it's a ZL1," he says with pride.

"It's beautiful." I know just how beautiful she is, inside and out. I've test driven one. She's the car of my dreams but way out of my price range. My dad always said I had champagne taste but only a beer budget. "Wait...I'm confused."

"The *bunny,* as you called it, belongs to my sister. And for the record, it's not a Rabbit, it's a Golf."

"Meh." I give him a teasing shrug. "Not much difference." He watches me, as I walk between the two cars, peeking through the tinted windows.

"I was changing the spark plugs for her in the afternoon and didn't have time to switch cars back before I had to leave to meet you."

I turn to say something, but I lose my train of thought, when I see the look he's giving me. He takes a step toward me, causing me to back up until I can go no further. The air around us begins to sizzle with a new kind of energy. I swallow hard as it ignites every nerve ending in my body. Taking hold of my wrist, he lifts my hand and holds it firmly against the cold glass window.

Staring directly into my eyes, he follows suit with the other, anchoring them in place. When he brings his lips to mine, he pins me against the car with the weight of his lean, muscular body. My heart begins to pound, pumping heat through me so quickly that the chill of the frigid steel against my back quickly fades. I've never, in all my years, experienced a kiss like this before. What starts as a teasing, tender brush of his lips, finishes with a slow, desirous claiming of my mouth. With every exchange of breath, he deepens his kiss, exploring. Learning.

Angst and excitement whirl within me, driving out all rational thought. Something inexplicable draws me to this man, making me want to get closer. Now that I've experienced it, I know it will be dangerously addictive. Cool air sweeps across my lips as the warmth of his breath fades away. His slow withdrawal leaves me aching for more. I never want this to *expire*. When he releases his hold on me, I remain frozen with my hands against the glass. With my eyes closed, I try to fill my lungs back up with air. Roger takes a step back and opens my driver's side door. "You're going to be late."

I open my eyes at the sound of his voice. The chill of the air sobers me, bringing me back from my inflamed trance. I can't talk. I can't even think right now. Hell, it's all I can do to remember how to breathe.

A ghost of a smile spreads across his lips as he watches me peel myself off the side of the Camaro, still somewhat dazed. "They'll be looking for you back at the office." He steps to the side to let me pass. My brain races to think of a way to get out of work for the afternoon and experience that kiss again. He brushes his fingers across my cheek, trailing them down to my lips. "You need to get going," he prompts, when I hesitate. I stare into his piercing blue eyes, before I reluctantly give in. When I'm safely seated, he shuts me in.

"Lock your doors," he instructs through the closed window. "Text me when you're back in your office."

Chapter Seven

"So?" Jen asks, hanging on my every word.

"Mr. Ford turned it up a notch." I blush involuntarily.

Jen squeals. "Score one for the *nice* guy."

I start to tell her about the goodbye kiss and have to stop to fan my face with my hand.

"And then?"

"I went back to work in wet panties."

"Yuck." She wrinkles her nose. "That's not what I wanted to know. Did you hear from him last night?"

"His family took him out for dinner to celebrate his birthday. He messaged me later in the evening to say goodnight."

"Well, at least he let you know he was thinking about you."

I nod. "I'm stopping by his place tonight on my way home."

Jen looks at me shocked.

"He has to be home for his daughter tonight, so I'm going to go there."

"Ohhhh." She raises her eyebrows. "So you're meeting his daughter. Are you nervous?"

I pause a moment to think about it. "Should I be? She's only seven."

"Has he met the boys yet?"

"No."

"Are you going to introduce him to the boys?"

"I haven't decided yet."

"You're afraid."

"Well, yeah. It's kind of premature."

Jen purses her lips then gives me a reassuring smile. "You're still worried that he's going to exp..." She stops herself. "...disappear."

I shrug, afraid that saying it out loud will make it come true.

♥

"Damn you, Jennifer," I grumble to myself, as I pull into the driveway of Rogers semi-detached home in Brampton. I wasn't nervous before, but now she's got me thinking this is a bad idea. The curtains in the front window sway and I know that I'm being watched. When the front door swings open and Roger steps out onto the porch, my heart flutters. He smiles and moves to open my car door.

"I'm having a little bit of anxiety about this," I admit, as I accept his outstretched hand.

"Why? She's going to love you. Besides, all that matters is that I want to be with you."

I take in a deep breath and let it out slowly. "You'd think so, but believe me, if your friends and family don't like the person you're dating, it isn't going to last."

He scowls at me. "Why would you say that?"

"Uh, because it's true. Especially your kids. You haven't got any chance if the kids hate you."

He looks at me as if I've just imparted some profound wisdom on him.

"Have your kids hated any of the guys you've dated in the past?"

He guides my coat off my shoulders and hangs it in the front hallway closet. "I haven't had any long-term, committed relationships after my divorce. I've had *friends* that I dated casually, now and then, but I never introduced them to my kids."

"Hmmm." He starts to say something, but he's distracted by the pair of brilliant blue eyes curiously peeking around the corner. "Don't look now, but you're being watched," he confirms. Taking my hand, he leads me around the corner and into the family room. "Molly, this is Victoria."

She looks so...small. Retreating to the opposite side of the room, she leans against the large armchair in the corner, never taking her eyes off me.

"Hi, Molly," I offer, with a polite smile. "You can call me Tori."

"I'm sorry," Roger says, embarrassed that she's ignoring me.

"It's okay," I assure him. "Give her time."

And we do. Three hours worth of time. Despite our gentle prompting to get her engaged in conversation, she remains silent. Roger looks at me several times apologetically and I smile, trying to put him at ease. This is nothing. Wait until he has to meet my kids. If we get that far.

I'd be lying if I said I wasn't relieved when it was time for her to go to bed. While Roger tends to the ritual bedtime routine, I make myself comfortable on the couch and wait.

I'm flipping through movie choices when he joins me in the family room.

"Is everything okay?"

"All good." He hands me a glass and sits beside me. "It's Jameson and ginger ale."

I smile, pleased that he remembered that from our conversation the other night.

"Listen, Tori. I'm really sorry about Mo."

I wave it off. "Don't worry about it."

"It's hard. *Really* hard at times."

"Can I ask what happened to her mother?"

"She decided family life wasn't for her. She pretty much abandoned her. Just...*left*."

"I'm sorry," I say, sadly.

"It's okay. What about you? Why haven't you had a relationship since you're divorce?"

Good question. I let out a small sigh. "Well, I guess it's because none of the men I kept company with, was the *right* guy. And I really didn't want to get into another relationship just because it would have made my life *easier*."

He nods. "I get that. I've met a few women who made me think the same thing. One of the reasons I was so worried about online dating was bringing women home to meet Molly. There's a lot of crazy out there and I didn't want to expose her to any of it. She's so fragile right now."

I'm not eager to discuss the other women he's dating. At least not at the moment. There's something else on my mind. "Do you know what I've been thinking?" I ask with a playful smile.

"No clue."

"I've been thinking about *that* kiss."

"Kiss?"

"Uh, yeah. The kiss. At Lunch."

"Oh, **that** kiss." He tries to hide his amusement. "Well, there was really nothing special about that kiss," he teases.

"Okay, if you say so." I try to be coy about it, but I can't keep my eyes off his lips. Lips that seem to be getting closer. Lips that are calling me. It just got really warm in here. "Maybe you should kiss me again. Just so I can be sure that there's nothing special about your kisses."

"Maybe I should." He laughs at the sight of my puckered lips. Then all frivolity comes to an end. Leaning in, he claims me with the sensual caress of his lips. Time stands still while his hand travels up my leg, and his thumb brushes along my inner thigh. My arms wrap around him, pulling him in. When he cups my breast in his hand, through my shirt, he lets out a small growl. It inspires me, and like a horny high school girl, I shift my weight and straddle him, forcing him to sit back. I feel him swell and grow beneath me, as his hands find their way under my shirt and travel along bare skin.

Hungry for more of him, I lower my mouth to his. Passion takes over. Before I can blink, he lifts me off his lap and lays me down. Gently, he lowers himself, easing his body on top of mine. Chest to chest. Torso to torso. As he nibbles down my neck, he presses his hips forward and rubs his hard cock against me. My body responds, making me squirm beneath him. Grabbing the bottom of my shirt, he pulls it off over my head. All I can think of at this moment is getting him naked and inside me. Pausing, Roger glances over at the stairs, then down at my red lace bra. Without warning, he gets to his feet looking mortified.

Fear washes over me and I quickly sit up. I glance over the back of the couch expecting to see Molly standing there. I'm relieved to see that she's not, but she could have been.

"We could go upstairs to your room," I suggest, still feeling all wired up.

"I'm sorry." He passes me my shirt and sits beside me, leaving a few inches of space between us. "I don't want you to think all I'm interested in is sex."

I put my shirt back on and try to get my head around what just happened. "You do like sex, right?" I search for clarification.

"Yes, I like sex. I like sex a lot! But...Victoria, I'm falling for you and I don't want to rush into it."

I reach over and pinch his arm, making him flinch.

"Ouch, what was that for?"

"Just checking to see if you're real."

"Yeah, I'm for real."

"Well, I can honestly say that's something I'm not used to." I pick up the remote and hand it to him. "Alright then. You pick. No chick flicks."

"What's wrong with chick flicks?" he asks curiously.

"Not my thing. Let's just say if somebody isn't getting blown up, I'm out."

"Got it. Can I get you anything?"

I tip my head playfully, from one side to the other, while I think about it. "Cold shower. Dry panties."

He smiles, extremely proud of himself. "I meant a snack or something to drink."

"Oh, well, now I'm embarrassed."

He settles on *Smokey and the Bandit*, then places the remote down in front of him. I find it hard to take my eyes off him.

"What?" he finally asks.

"This is one of my favorite movies."

"Mine, too."

I have a sudden burst of excitement. "Do you remember the nickname Bandit gives her?"

"Fox. No wait, that ain't right. Fish!" he blurts out.

I burst into uncontrollable laughter.

"I take it that's wrong."

"It's..." I try to compose myself, but I can't help it. "It's Frog," I giggle. Good Lord, what's wrong with me? I hate giggling girls.

"Right. Because she's always jumping around in the front seat."

"YES!"

"I remember now." He begins to sing the theme song and I join in. How could I not? I don't think either of us hits any of the right notes or remembers all the words. It doesn't seem to matter. He reaches over and holds my hand, caressing his thumb across it and giving a gentle squeeze from time to time. For the first time, in a long time, I feel...happy.

♥

All the way home, I think about Molly. There's a troubled little girl behind those deep blue eyes. I sense it. Her silence is proof of it. I can't imagine how confused she must feel, seeing another woman in her home. As a mother, I can't imagine leaving her behind. I find myself wondering what it is I don't know. What must have happened to cause a mother to walk away and abandon her child? I've got enough life experience under my belt to know that I'm only getting one side of the story, and let's be honest, Roger's been rather vague about the whole thing so far.

To be fair, we are still practically strangers, and I haven't been forthcoming about my past either. It's only been a few days since our first date, but it seems a lot longer.

Chapter Eight

The late afternoon sun shines brightly through my office window, giving the illusion it's warm outside. Despite that, the bitter Canadian winter wind blows through the poorly insulated windows, making it feel like I'm sitting in an igloo. Roger is scheduled to work evenings this week, so I haven't seen him for a couple of days. Last night, when he had time during the evening, he sent me a picture. I opened it expecting to find his usual romantic couple cuddling. What he sent made me fan my face instead. I asked for *more*, and he accepted the challenge. Game on! Luckily, I'm busy at work today, so it keeps my mind occupied while he's at home sleeping.

I pick up my phone to read an incoming text.

Roger: Are you busy?
Tori: Always. What's up?
Roger: I'm outside.

I practically jump to my feet and look out the window. My excitement heightens at the sight of his Camaro. I type as I make my way to the lobby.

Tori: I'm on my way out.

The cold air hits me hard when I walk out the front doors. I was so excited to see him that I didn't think about the temperature. Roger meets me mid-way in the parking lot with his coat held open in front of him.

"Jesus, woman, what were you thinking? It's not summer." He wraps his jacket around me and ushers me to the car.

I settle into the luxuriously heated seat as Roger takes his place on the other side.

"What are you doing here?"

"I brought you a tea." He points at the takeaway cup in the holder.

"Shouldn't you be sleeping?" I ask concerned.

"Nah., I got enough sleep. I start work in a few hours anyway." There's a boyish grin on his face as he watches me take a cautious sip of the hot tea and place it back in the holder. "I couldn't stand the thought of not seeing you another day."

My heart flutters. "Oh, that was smooth."

"I'm not trying to be smooth; I'm just saying the truth."

"I'm glad you're here."

"Do you like Boston cream donuts?"

"I do."

He unfolds the top of the paper bag and slides it out. "I thought you might."

I'm amused. "Oh? And why is that?"

"Because we seem to have a lot in common." He takes a bite and then passes it to me. I can't resist, I poke my tongue into the middle and lick at the cream filling.

"Hmmm. It appears you have a very talented tongue." He adjusts the way he's sitting, and if I have to guess, it's because he needs some slack in his trousers for what's starting to go on in there.

"That, I do." I lick my lips. "Every girl should have a skill. Mine's not cooking." I hand it back to him and watch as he pushes the rest of it into his mouth.

He chews twice and then swallows. "Good to know." He glances at the time on the dashboard. "I guess you have to get going."

"Yes," I confirm with regret. Why is it so hard to leave him?

"If I kiss you goodbye will everybody in the office be watching out the window."

"Definitely." I stare at his lips.

"Do you care?"

"Not at all."

The sun shines on his face through the driver's side window. His blue eyes sparkle so brightly that it makes the high-gloss finish on his Camaro look like flat black. As he leans toward me, I close my eyes and wait...and wait.

"Fucking console," he grumbles.

I open one eye and peek at him. He points down at the monstrosity between us. "Whoever designed this obviously didn't think this through."

"Where there's a will, there's a way." I want this kiss so badly that I'll mount this console like a pommel horse if I have to. I lean over as far as I can, then grab hold of Roger's shirt, and pull him in until his mouth bumps into mine.

His fingers gently brush across my cheek as his lips press against mine. I close my eyes and let the warmth of him wash over me with every teasing lick of his tongue. The loud piercing sound of the car horn startles me as Roger adjusts his position, trying to get closer.

I pull away, laughing.

"If they weren't watching out the window before, they are now," he says embarrassed.

"I guess I should get back to work. Thank you for the tea."

"Just hold on."

Roger is around the car in a flash. "I'll walk you to the door." He extends his hand.

Safely in the warmth of the foyer, he slides his jacket off my shoulders. "Can I call you later?"

"I'll be disappointed if you don't." I suddenly become aware of the coworkers peeking around corners.

"Great." He holds my hand for a long moment. "Well, take care."

"Take care?"

"Yeah," he says looking uncomfortable. "Have a great afternoon."

"Okay, I will. You too. Call me if you get a chance."

He nods as he pushes open the heavy glass doors into the parking lot. Schoolyard teasing erupts from the customer service room next door. "Alright, alright. Knock it off, this isn't kindergarten."

♥

Jen calls my cell, while I'm on my way home.

"Hey! How was Quebec City?"

"It's beautiful, I wish I had more time to sightsee and less time to work. How are you?"

"I'm good."

"And Roger? Is he still around?"

"Yeah, he is. It's a miracle, eh?"

"Not really, Tori. You're an awesome woman. I wish you'd stop selling yourself short."

"I'm not. It's just that...well, you know."

"Think positive."

"I am. I'm positive I'm going to fuck it up somehow."

"Well, I can understand your concern. It's not easy being in a brand new relationship at this time of the year."

"Relationship? Do you really think this qualifies as a relationship already? I don't even know if he's seeing other women."

"Maybe you should ask him that."

"It would be awkward if he says yes."

"Even more awkward if you make plans for Valentine's Day, and he's spending the day with somebody else."

"Valentine's Day?" I repeat.

"What is wrong with you? Yes, Valentine's Day. It's in a few weeks."

"Shit." My car starts to make a horrible sound and lights start to flash on the dashboard.

"Tori? Are you okay?"

"Yes, sorry. Something's wrong with my car."

"Do you need to call the auto club?"

"No, it's still running."

"So what are you going to do about Valentine's Day?"

"I'm not going to worry about it. Who knows if he'll still be around then? Listen, I'm glad you're home safe, I'm going to phone Tanner and see if he knows what's wrong with my car."

"Okay, sweetie. Let me know that you make it home safe."

I disconnect the call and request that my virtual assistant get Tanner on the phone. It rings several times before he answers.

"Sup?"

"Hey, there's something wrong with my car."

"What?"

"It's making funny sounds."

"Like what?"

"There was like a loud 'pop' then it sounded kind of like a chortle...then *rrr rrr rr*," I pause, waiting for the burst of laughter to subside. "Very funny, take me off speaker phone, please."

"Sorry, I couldn't resist. The guys are all impressed with your interpretive troubleshooting skills."

"I bet. Any idea what it is?"

"Did any of the dash lights come on?"

"Yeah, but they went off again and I don't remember which ones they were."

"Is it still running?"

"Yes."

"What does the temperature gauge read?"

"It's not overheating. It's just driving really sluggish."

"Okay, so pull over and make sure that you've got engine oil and rad fluid in it before you drive it all the way home."

"Okay, got it."

I pull off the busy highway onto one of the less travelled country roads and put on my four ways. I use an old towel to remove the cap and check the dipstick. Everything looks okay but better safe than sorry, I figure, as I dump in the extra container I carry in the trunk.

♥

I jump when Tanner tosses my keys at me. "What was wrong with it?"

"There aren't any engine lights on. I couldn't find anything wrong with it, other than it had too much oil in it."

"That's weird." I try to look innocent but I'm pretty sure he's on to me.

"Maybe you put shitty gas in it, and it choked up for a bit. Drop it off at the garage after work tomorrow, and I'll do full diagnostics and run an engine cleaner through it."

"Thank you, Tanner." I look down at my phone.

Roger: Are you home yet?
Tori: Yes.

I answer it on the first ring.

"Sorry, I forgot."

"That's okay, I was worried."

"How's work?" I flip through all the store flyers while we talk, looking at all the Valentine's Day sales.

"It's work. It gets crazy around here some days."

"I know the feeling." I toss the pile of papers aside. "Hey. Can I ask you a question?"

"Sure," he answers apprehensively.

"Are you seeing anyone else?"

"No."

I have to admit, hearing him say that puts me more at ease, but I've inadvertently looked over at his phone a few times and seen message notifications come up from the dating site. "So, are you still *shopping*?"

"Shopping? Tori, I'm a guy. I have no idea what you're talking about," he says, confused.

"Shopping for other girls. On the dating site."

"No."

"Are you seeing other guys?" You just never know these days so I might as well rule that out, too.

"Absolutely not," he says, appalled. "Why are you asking? Are you seeing other people?" he asks, nervously.

"No. I told you, I deleted my account. We haven't really talked about seeing other people. That's perfectly okay, if you are," I add, rambling. I'm saying it out loud, but I'll be crushed if he admits that he's playing the field. "That's what dating is, right? Going out with different people until you find the right one." There's a long pause and it makes my pulse pound a little faster.

"I'm not interested in seeing anybody else. Just you," he confirms.

I take a relieved breath. "You have no idea how glad I am to hear that," I admit. "I just didn't want things to get awkward over Valentine's Day."

"Oh." I can hear the uneasy tone in his voice. "About that. I'm not going to be in town that weekend."

"Perfect. Then we don't have to worry about it."

"I'm sorry. I made plans a long time ago to attend an out of town concert with my buddy, Johnnie."

"No really, it's okay," I assure him. "We've only been together for a few weeks. It's probably better that way. Then there are no embarrassing moments if someone gets all romantic and mushy when the other person isn't quite there yet."

"Do you want, romantic and mushy?"

"No," I lie. "It's not a big deal."

"I don't think you're telling me the truth."

"Nah, Valentine's Day has never been a special day for me."

"You deserve to be treated special every day, not just one day a year."

That was a promise my ex made me, but it didn't quite work out that way. I think I need a subject change.

"Hey, is tomorrow your day off?"

"Yeah, why?"

"I was wondering if you could do me a huge favor?"

"Anything."

"I need to drop my car off at the garage Tanner works at. It was doing some weird things on the way home tonight, and he's going to check it out."

"Would you like me to take a look at it?"

YES! "No. But thank you. Tanner's kind of struggling to find his place right now. You know? Not a kid, but not quite a man yet, either. I just seem to be adding to his anxiety. If I was to let you look at it, he'd think I don't trust him to fix it."

"It's a difficult time in a boy's life."

"Thank you for understanding. Could you follow me to the shop, just outside of town, to drop it off? I'll need a ride home."

"My mom is taking Molly to dance tomorrow night, so I can do that."

"Thank you, I'll meet you at your house after work and you can follow me from there."

"See you then."

"Good night."

"Victoria..."

The sound of my name coming from his lips makes me shiver. Or maybe I'm just coming down with something. "Yes?"

"If I could change my plans for Valentine's Day, I would do it for you."

Chapter Nine

When I pull up in front of Roger's home, in the north end of Brampton, his mother is just leaving. I'm thankful for the slow-moving traffic today since Molly glares at me out the window as they pass by. Roger is putting the garbage to the end of the road and seeing him makes me smile. I pull into the driveway and roll down the window. "Hey there! Let's get going before the rush hour traffic gets too bad."

He takes his keys out of his back pocket. "I'm ready. Lead the way."

"If I lose you, just text me."

He laughs. "You're not going to lose me."

"Okay, Ford. Keep up."

I head out into traffic, watching to make sure that he's behind me. City driving always makes me crazy. The constant stopping and starting. Grrrr. Twatwaffle commuters, who don't know how to drive, just about send me over the edge daily.

Luckily, we have a short distance to travel before we break free of the city congestion and hit the open road. When we make the last turn out of the city it feels like a heavy weight is lifted off my chest...and lands on my foot. When there's nothing in front of me, I'm not happy unless I'm accelerating. Roger is right behind me, keeping pace at a safe distance. My car might be old, but she moves. We maneuver the scenic Forks Of The Credit backroads like a familiar lover, easing into the hairpin turns and pushing her limits through the hills and valleys. Before I know it, we're pulling into the driveway of the garage where Tanner works part-time.

I've barely put it in park when my door swings open, startling me. Roger takes hold of my wrist and pulls me to my feet. Before I can say a single word, he claims my mouth in a passionate kiss. My hands slide inside his open jacket and across his chest. I can feel the adrenaline-fueled pounding of his heart. When his primal possession begins to fade, I pull away, shocked and breathless.

"Leave the keys on the front seat!" Tanner yells from one of the bay doors. "I'll drive it home later."

Roger releases me and shakes his head. "Is there anything you need out of your car, Danica Patrick?"

I shrug playfully, trying not to smirk. "Nope, I'm all good."

He opens the passenger door of the Camaro and ushers me in.

"Can I drive?" I ask optimistically.

"Not a chance," he chuckles.

I love the rumble of the eight-cylinder engine. Taking the backroads home, he avoids stoplights and traffic. I enjoy every moment of the drive until Roger gets curious.

"So, can I ask why you left your husband?"

I pause, not really wanting to have this conversation. "You don't really want to know all about my baggage."

"I don't?"

"No, you don't."

"Hey, we all have baggage. When you meet someone you want to be with, you talk to each other, and you help each other downsize that full-size baggage into carry-on size."

Fair point. "My ex was a very unhappy man. So unhappy that he became angry. I couldn't fix it."

He draws a breath and then releases it before he speaks. "Did he hurt you?"

I bite my lip and choose not to answer.

He glances at me briefly while he's driving. "I'm sorry."

"It's okay." My hands fidget in my lap.

Roger doesn't push it any further. He's already figured me out. I watch his silhouette in the dark, waiting for that moment when his face is illuminated by the light of a passing car. The sight of his strong jawline and masculine profile makes me get a little twitchy.

I'm not sure if he planned it, or if it's a coincidence, but the songs that play, one after another, on the current playlist are all my favorites. I try to ignore the internal struggle taking place within me but it's strong and I feel the need to touch him. Turning sideways, I reach over the console and rub my hand across his knee, gently squeezing. He takes a deep breath and tries to focus on driving. I like the warmth of his body. I want to explore further up his thigh, but the damn console is in the way. "Do you want to pull over?"

He turns his head quickly, shocked at my suggestion. I seem to shock him a lot.

"What?"

I comb my fingers through his hair and trace his ear with my index finger. "I'm sure we can find a spot to pull over on one of these dark country roads." The thought excites me. "Roger?" I prompt him to answer.

He glances over at me with a look of temptation that almost makes me laugh out loud.

"No."

"No?" I place my hand on his shoulder and caress downward. I can see his tightly clenched jaw as we pass under an isolated streetlight.

"No. We're not teenagers."

"Come on, admit it. You're tempted," I tease.

"I am."

"AHA! I knew it."

"You're forgetting something." He points down toward the console. "Unless you're a contortionist, I can't see how it's happening."

I wrench my neck to see in the back seat only to be disappointed by the clutter there.

"Sorry, I didn't have time to clean it out."

I shrug. "We're only a few blocks from my home anyway."

♥

Roger pulls up in front of the house and I find myself feeling that same sense of dread. I don't want to leave. "If you're not doing anything the weekend after Johnnie and I get back, I'd like you to come to dinner with me and Molly to meet my parents."

What did he just say? I hesitate. "Sure. I'd like that."

Roger grins. "Then why do you look like you're going to throw up?"

I wipe the perspiration from my forehead. "It got really warm in here."

Roger looks at me with concern as I try to figure out what I want to say. It's frustrating that I tend to babble when I'm around him.

"Are you sure you want me to meet your parents so soon?"

"Why not?"

I'm not sure I want to explain it. "I'm afraid. It's just that..."

"You can tell me anything," he assures me.

"I haven't really had to meet parents in the past. Before it got to that point, my relationships..."

He lowers his brow, looking at me concerned. "Just say it."

"They expire," I say, feeling embarrassed.

"Expire?"

The confusion on his face makes me sigh. "Yes. For some reason, we get that far and they...disappear: vanish." I frown. "I have a three date expiry."

"I see," he sits sideways, staring at me. "I do believe we're past four dates."

"Well, yes," I argue. "But they all happened in the first week. Things are moving pretty quickly. In normal dating, if we dated once a week, let's say...then the fourth date would be about four weeks in. And we've known each other...almost four weeks!" The situation has me wound pretty tightly, and I'm annoyed that he looks amused.

"You've given this a lot of thought."

"Don't make fun of me," I warn.

"So you think I'm going to disappear?"

I realize now, how stupid the whole thing sounds. Still, the thought is constantly on my mind. I lower my head and remain silent. Roger reaches down and stills my fidgeting hands. When I fail to acknowledge him, he tips my chin with his finger until I turn toward him. Roger presses his lips against mine for a long slow kiss. When I open my eyes, he gently brushes my hair away from my face.

"I'm not going anywhere. I'm in for the long haul."

There's a moment in a girl's life when she realizes...*This is it. He's the one.* The moment when time stands still and everything goes quiet, except for the sound of two souls coming together and celebrating. For me, that moment occurs under the soft glow of the front porch light, in the front seat of a Chevy Camaro ZL1.

I'm not ready for him to leave. "Do you want to come in?"

He checks the time before he agrees.

I stumble over shoes reaching for the light switch. "I guess nobody's home."

Roger follows me into the family room and takes a seat on the couch. I turn on the TV, but it doesn't matter what's on because I have no intention of watching it. I nibble on his ear then continue down his neck.

"What are you doing to me?"

"I thought we could fool around a little."

"What if the boys come home?"

"The light in the backyard is on a sensor. We'll see it come on."

Roger glances at the back door and then down at my lips. It doesn't take too much convincing. In moments, we're engaged in a passionate make-out session like a couple of teenagers. Roger unbuttons my shirt and releases my breasts from my pink satin bra. He makes a low growling sound as he lowers his face to my chest.

I close my eyes and enjoy the warmth of his mouth on them. Adjusting my position to give him better access, I open my eyes and notice the back porch light go on. I sit up quickly and grab the blanket beside me, startling the hell out of Roger. I cover us both, just in the nick of time, as Dallas opens the door and comes up the steps.

"Hey!" I try to make it look innocent. "How was your day?"

"Alright."

He looks between us, and I'm pretty sure he knows what was going on a few minutes before he walked in. My face turns a bright shade of red. "Dallas, this is my friend, Roger."

"How's it going?" Roger asks from the couch, unable to get to his feet for a proper introduction.

Dallas kicks his boots off, looking unimpressed. "I'm good."

"We're gonna hang out down here and watch a movie," I advise.

"Keep your hands off my mother, fucktard," he growls halfway up the stairs.

I put my hand over my mouth, shocked. Roger stiffens beside me and leans his head back against the couch. "Well, that's not the way I wanted to meet your kids."

I burst out laughing. "He'll get over it."

"He'll probably hate me forever now."

"I doubt that."

"I better get going."

"Really?" I'm disappointed it spoiled the mood. "What worse could happen now?" I tease.

"A lot worse. You have a way of getting me all riled up."

"I do?" The thought of that makes me happy.

Under the blanket, Roger takes my hand and places it on his hard cock. "Any more silly questions?"

I give it a gentle rub on the outside of his trousers and smile when it twitches. "Nope, I get it now."

"Seriously, I should go and pick up Molly. She's been struggling with her schoolwork this week."

How do I keep the man away from his daughter? It's a very selfish thing for me to do. I get to my feet, intending to walk him to the door. Excruciating pain shoots through my leg as I put my weight on it. It pulses through my entire body, making me feel sick to my stomach. Perspiration dots my forehead as Roger reaches out for me.

"Are you okay?"

His voice sounds distorted like he's in a wind tunnel or way off in the distance.

"Sit down!" I hear him say. "Victoria!" He forces me back onto the couch and crouches down in front of me. "Are you okay? Talk to me. What's going on?"

The pain eases up a little and I find my voice. "I'm sorry. I'm okay."

"You don't look okay to me, what the fuck is going on?"

"On the shelf, beside the microwave, in the kitchen there's a pill bottle. Could you get it for me, please?"

He looks down at my trembling hands and nods, responding quickly.

I take off the lid and dump two in my hand. He hands me an open bottle of water and I use it to wash them down.

"Now, would you tell me what's going on? Those are extremely powerful nerve blockers you've just taken."

"How did you know that?"

"I used to play competitive hockey; I've had my share of injuries."

I can feel him staring at me, waiting for an explanation. "One night, my ex came home drunk. Something I did made him angry, and when I tried to walk away, he reached out to grab me. I lost my balance and fell down the stairs."

"Jesus."

I choose not to tell him that the doctor said I could have been paralyzed. "I have permanent nerve damage that affects my back, from my hip down into my leg. They said that I'll never be free from the pain. I forgot to take my meds tonight."

"You know, if I ever meet this man, it's very likely that I might kill him."

Chapter Ten

I unpack a bag of groceries onto Roger's kitchen counter. "Really, you don't have to do this," he insists.

"I want to."

"Are you feeling up to it?"

"Yes, I'm fine."

"You mentioned that you didn't sleep very well."

"Nightmares. Sometimes I think the side effects of the meds are worse than the pain I'm taking them for."

"I highly doubt it. I've seen that pain on your face. It was terrifying."

"I'm sorry. I wish I could manage the pain better without them. They're ridiculously expensive and some of the side effects never went away for me. On top of the nightmares, I get random bouts of nausea and anxiety and still have to deal with the pain at times. The boys are all out this evening, so there's no reason for me to rush home."

"Okay, if you want to."

"I do. Now, while I cook dinner, you and Molly can start making dessert."

"I love dessert. What are we making?"

"Brownies."

"Oh," he says, looking mortified. "I'm not really a dessert chef."

I laugh, "You don't need to be." I reach for the box on the counter. "Just add water."

"You're my kinda girl. Hey, Mo! Can you come in here for a minute?" When she doesn't reply, he looks at me and frowns. "Molly?" he calls out louder.

"Maybe she has the headphones plugged in," I suggest.

Roger leaves the kitchen and returns a few minutes later with seven-year-old Molly glued to his side.

"There you are." I give her a friendly smile. "I need some reinforcements here, Molly. Your dad tells me he's not a very good baker, and I have these brownies that we need to make for dessert. Can you help?"

I hold out the mixing bowl and a wooden spoon. She leaves me hanging for a very long time, making me nervous. I think Roger holds his breath until she reaches up and takes them from me. "Awesome! Thank you."

She climbs up on a kitchen chair while Roger reads the directions on the back of the box. I finish adding the rest of the ingredients into the sauce and check on their progress.

"How's it going?" I laugh out loud at the sight of him. "How in the heck did you get batter all over you?"

"I don't know," he grunts. "I told you, I'm not good at this stuff."

"If there's any batter left in the bowl, let's get it into the oven."

I grab the dishcloth and clean the mess off the table while Roger hoses Molly off at the sink. "Do you want to help me set the table?" I hope that including her will help draw her out of her shell.

Without a word, she shakes her head. Roger wipes the last bit of brownie batter out of her curls. "You can go finish watching your show until dinner's ready."

When she's out of the room, he gives me an apologetic look.

"She does talk, right?"

"Yes, but not much. Her teachers are a little worried. I've tried counseling with her, but that hasn't helped much either."

"Well, if it's any consolation, I have the opposite problem. My youngest is acting out in class. The boy is brilliant, but he spends most of the day in the principal's office for disrupting class."

"Really?"

"Yes, I'm sure it's because he's bored and not challenged enough. The guidance counselors let him drop his courses from academic to applied without consulting me."

"Why would they do that?"

"It's his choice. It's high school and he's an adult, according to them. He doesn't need my permission or my approval."

"That doesn't seem right." He wraps his arms around me from behind. "Mmmm, that smells really good. What's it called?"

I have a momentary lapse of memory as I enjoy the warmth of his body against mine and his strong masculine arms banded around me. "Ummm, spaghetti."

"Huh. I always thought spaghetti came out of a can."

We both burst into laughter. "Set the table, please."

He grabs the utensils off the counter and turns to find Molly standing behind us in the kitchen.

"Hey, Mo," he says, surprised.

I turn to meet the icy glare of her blue eyes.

"Are you hungry?" I ask as I serve up a small bowl.

She nods her head. I smile, pleased with the progress we're making. At least she's acknowledging me now. "Where do you sit?"

She points to the chair closest to the sliding glass doors and I promptly place her bowl there. Glancing over at Roger, I catch him smiling.

I ask Molly about school and dance, hoping that I can coax her into a conversation. Roger reminds her, gently, that when someone is talking to her, she needs to answer. Still, I find myself changing my approach and asking questions that require a nod or shake of the head. Baby steps.

I'm not sure which one of us makes the most mess, but judging from the sauce all over Molly's face, she enjoyed it. The timer on the stove makes me jump when it sounds off loudly.

Molly spreads the icing on the brownies and watches it melt from the heat. When she's completely covered the top, Roger cuts them into squares and puts one on each of our plates.

"Are they supposed to be this...chewy?" Roger asks, with his mouth full.

"I don't think so. Did you follow the directions?" I ask, trying to swallow. He looks at me confused and shrugs.

"Can I have a glass of milk, please?" Molly asks, trying to pry a wad of dough from the roof of her mouth with her tongue.

I laugh at the expression on her face and get to my feet. "I think we all need one to wash these down."

"I want my daddy to get it."

"Molly," Roger scolds. "Don't be rude."

I put three glasses on the table and shake my head discreetly. He lets out a frustrated breath, but I know he understands my thoughts. Taking the jug out of my hand, he pours all three glasses of milk.

By the time Roger returns from tucking her into bed, I've cleaned up and done the dishes. He rewards me with a kiss.

"You know, I'm working the next two nights."

"Yes, I know."

"Then I'm going away for the weekend, for the concert."

"Right. The *I hate Valentine's Day* diversion," I mumble, as I try to walk away.

Roger reaches out, stopping me. "You know that I made those plans a long time ago."

"I know. I'm sorry. It doesn't really matter. It's just a day."

He laughs once. "Right. I know it's important to you girls."

"We've seen each other every day for the past two weeks. You probably need a break from me."

"Why would you say that?"

I shrug, trying to convey indifference but he knows better.

♥

I lie in bed watching TV until later in the morning. I try not to be disappointed, but it sucks. Ten years of being single on Valentine's Day, after a twelve-year marriage to a man who didn't think I was worth the effort. And now I've met someone who makes me feel beautiful, safe...and wanted, and he has other plans with the boys. I really don't feel like it, but I drag myself out of bed and get dressed. I'd rather stay in bed, feeling sorry for myself all day.

My phone rings and I look down to see Roger's name. I hesitate, thinking that maybe I'll blow him off for now. I know it's immature and selfish of me, but I really don't want to hear about the wonderful time he's having. On the fourth ring, I decide that I want to hear his voice.

"Hey."

"Hi, there," he says cheerfully.

"Are you on your way?"

"Yeah, sort of."

"If you get a chance, let me know you're there safely."

"Victoria. I'm there safely."

"You are? I'm confused."

He chuckles. "You know I'd rather be spending time with you this weekend."

"Yes, I know. But this is one of your favorite bands, and you've had plans with your friends for a long time before I came along."

"Where are you?"

"Upstairs, why?"

"Look out the hall window."

I wander to the end of the hall and stare out the window that overlooks the backyard and the parking lane. "What am I looking for?"

A thrill runs through me at the sight of him rounding the neighbors' garage and entering my gate. He's carrying with him the largest bouquet of flowers I've ever seen in my life. He glances up at me standing in the window and smiles.

I'm down the stairs and out the back door before he reaches the porch. By the time I throw my arms around him, I'm starting to tear up. "You came all the way out here to see me before you go?"

"No. I came all the way out here to pick you up and take you away for the night."

I pull myself away from him, confused. "You what?"

"I made arrangements for us to spend the night at the Royal Harbour Resort in Thornbury. It's one of my favorite places, and I thought you might appreciate a night away from the kids. Just you and me."

"What about your concert? Your friends?"

Roger waves his hand in the air, in a dismissive manner. "I told them I wanted to spend today with you, and they understood. Don't pinch me."

"Okay, I won't this time. How about a kiss instead?"

"I like that idea much better."

Me too. I gently place my lips on his and caress my fingers through his hair. His hand glides across my hip and around my back, pulling me closer. The large bouquet of flowers stops him from surrounding me in a full embrace. I pull myself away when it finally sinks in what he's just said.

Roger guides me into the house. "Let's get these flowers in water. How quickly can you pack an overnight bag?"

"Not long. What exactly do I need?"

He senses my hesitation. "Tori, I have no hidden agenda for this weekend, other than to spend some time together without kids around. There's no plan to seduce you or strings attached. The room has two double beds."

That's Roger Ford, he does everything with an annoying degree of chivalry and formality. I nod in agreement, but I'm not entirely sure that's what I want. These days, my thoughts are consumed with him. He's the cliché...first thing I think of every morning and the last thing on my mind every night.

I toss a change of clothes in a duffle bag, then open a dresser drawer to get something to sleep in. I pull out a slinky little nightie, then think twice about it, and grab a T-shirt and pair of shorts instead. I start to experience a little bit of anxiety as I try to figure out everything I might need for overnight.

"How ya doing?" He laughs.

His voice startles me, making me jump. I turn to find him leaning against the doorjamb, watching me.

"Do I need something fancy?"

"Fancy?"

"Yeah." I hand him the bag to hold while I stuff a few personal items inside. "Are we going out at all, for dinner or anything?"

"Would you prefer we order in?"

"No." Actually, I would. This is about the umpteenth time that I've thought this is a bad idea since he got here. "I just need to know if I should pack a dress and pretty shoes."

"Mmm." He takes a long slow look down my body. "Yes. I think you should."

My face turns red, and I quickly try to put some space between us, while I find the perfect little black dress for the occasion.

"Done now?" he asks, smiling.

Still blushing, I avoid eye contact and zip up the bag. I try to take it out of his hand, but he tightens his grip. "I've got it," he insists.

On my way to his car, I text the boys to let them know that I'll be away until tomorrow. Now that they're older, I have a lot more freedom. Mind you, being raised by a single mom meant they had to become a lot more independent than most kids their age.

Roger tosses my bag into the back seat. As he rounds the front of the Camaro, I take a sneak peek into the bags back there. When he opens the door, he narrows his eyes. "What's the matter?" he asks concerned.

I point at the goods in the bag behind me.

"You've been snooping?"

"Sorry."

"Geesh, I thought girls loved surprises."

"Not this girl. I hate surprises."

"Apparently," he says, sounding a little disappointed. Now I feel bad for spoiling his fun.

"You planned all this?"

"Yes."

"For me?"

He stares at me for a long time, trying to work something out, while his eyes glimmer a more brilliant blue than usual.

"Yes. Because you're worth it." He smiles and playfully pinches my chin. "Ready?"

"Ready," I confirm.

Chapter Eleven

I love road trips. There's something therapeutic about a long drive in the country. Loud music adds to the healing powers of the warm sunlight. I've often wondered if I was a dog in another life because the gusting breeze against my face through my open window creates a vibrant energy inside me. If I *was* a dog, I'd be jumping back and forth between the seats and wagging my tail.

Roger glances over at me repeatedly with a look of contentment and it makes me suspicious. "What?"

"You're beautiful when the sun shines on you and lights up your face. Your eyes are the most stunning shade of green. It takes my breath away."

For someone who claims he has a habit of saying all the wrong things, he sure has a way of sayings things that sweep me off my feet. That's something new to me, and quite frankly, I have no clue how to respond.

His favorite song comes on the radio, and he turns up the volume until the rearview mirror vibrates. I love that he sings to me. He couldn't carry a tune in a bucket if his life depended on it, but it's the most beautiful music to me.

We're on the road for a little over two hours, but it seems to fly by quickly. The resort right on Georgian Bay looks like a lovely place to stay. It's certainly not the *No Tell Motel* scene that I'm used to. If anybody asked if I've ever experienced the type of motel that you can rent by the hour, I'd most certainly deny it.

This is certainly not one of those places. The foyer is beautifully decorated with shiny glass tiles and marble floors. There's a lovely sitting room off to the side with inviting leather chairs. I'm loving Mr. Ford's style.

As promised, the room has two double beds. While he unloads the bags from the baggage cart, I try to decide which one I'd prefer. It really doesn't matter to me, but he insists I pick. I toss my coat on the bed closest to the window and wonder just how this is going to work. I'm lost for a moment as I watch him turn down the thermostat.

"I forgot to tell you to bring a bathing suit." He opens the fridge and fills it with the beverages he's brought with him. "There's a pool and a hot tub." He gives me a boyish grin.

"Well luckily, I brought my bathing suit."

"Good girl," he says, pleased.

I sit on the edge of the bed, smiling. Funny how those two words don't sound creepy coming from Roger's lips. In fact, I think my vagina just twitched.

"Let's have a drink before we head down for dinner,"

He pours two very strong Jameson and ginger ales and puts them on the table by the window. Sitting in the large comfy side chair, he extends his hands and invites me onto his lap. If it wasn't sweltering in here before, it certainly is now that I'm sitting atop him with my side pressed against his muscular chest.

I need a drink. The Jameson goes down a little too smoothly, making him very chatty. I think I got the compressed version of his whole family history in a few short minutes.

"You haven't said much about your parents."

I tense a little, and he immediately releases me, letting me get to my feet. "My dad passed away a few years ago."

"I'm sorry."

I feel his eyes follow me as I move around the room.

"Were you close?"

I pick up my cup and empty it. "Yes."

"That must have been tough. Was he ill?"

"No. I wasn't expecting him to leave me so soon." Booze. I need more booze. I pick up Roger's glass and finish it, too, glancing at him over the edge as I do. The heat in the room, combined with the whiskey, starts to make me feel a little lightheaded. Roger senses my unease.

"And your mom?"

"Shortly after his death she ran into her high school sweetheart and they got married. She sold the house and they retired up north."

"Are you okay?" he asks, concerned when I stumble on a few of my words.

I try to break the tension with a small playful smile. "I'll be right back."

♥

When I come out of the bathroom wearing my little black dress, Roger has poured wine, lit candles, and has cued up his romantic date night playlist. The man is pulling out all the stops tonight. If his plan was to *not* seduce me tonight, he's failing. He holds out his hand.

"Dance with me."

My nerves grab a hold of me and my hand begins to tremble slightly. I take small, cautious steps in my heels, worried that my hip is going to give out and I'm going to fall and make an ass out of myself. Why is this suddenly so unnerving?

"I'm not really a good dancer," I admit, as he takes me into hold.

"Me neither," he confesses. "Basically, I'm just going to stand in the same spot here and sway."

I let out a small nervous laugh. "That's okay with me. I never learned how to follow. I always try to lead."

"There's a shocker."

"Hey!"

He chuckles and pulls me closer until I'm nestled against his chest. I'm still a little lightheaded from the booze. His arms band around me, firmly, keeping me steady. It's as if this is exactly where I'm meant to be, tucked in under his chin. The warmth of his breath on my head is calming.

He sways. "Victoria," he whispers softly.

"Yes."

"You haven't told me much about the things your ex-husband did to you, but I think I have a good idea."

I stiffen in his arms, and he presses his lips to the top of my head to try and settle me.

"I know that locking things up inside and building up walls is how you survived all these years."

I pull away and look up at him, not sure if I like where this is going.

"Acknowledging your feelings," he continues, "and talking about them makes you feel vulnerable and it's terrifying for you. I get it."

I look down to escape his gaze for a few moments, but he lifts my chin. "Sweetheart, at some point you need to let me in. *This guy*," he points to himself, "is never going to hurt you."

I struggle to keep my emotions in check but tears well up in my eyes.

"Sorry, I didn't mean to make you cry."

"I'm not crying."

He nods once, and pulls me closer, content to let it go *this time*. I'm not sure how many songs we sway to; I'm lost to everything around me except the beating of his heart. Pressed against his chest, the thrumming washes away the numbness I've known most of my life and makes me start to feel alive again. I can tell by the energy I just felt run through his body that he's feeling the same.

He loosens his grip a little. "We should think about going for dinner."

"Can we order room service? I don't really feel like going out."

"Are you sure? You look so beautiful; I thought you'd be disappointed if you didn't get to show off that dress."

I think about it for a moment, but I really don't want to leave. "I'm happy to stay here, just the two of us."

"Okay," he agrees, releasing me. "If you're sure, but you need to eat something before you fall over."

"I already looked through the room service menu and nothing really appealed to me."

"Pizza it is." He takes out his phone. "Anything you don't like on a pizza?"

"Pineapple and ham."

"Really? You're a Hawaiian hater?"

"I like pineapple. It just has no business on a pizza."

"Fair enough."

I turn on the TV and flip through the channels. "Why is it there are hundreds of shows on right now, and I can't find anything that interests me?"

"I have the same problem. Most of the time I end up turning it off and listening to music."

"Luckily we both like the same kind of music."

"Why does that matter?"

"What chance does a heavy metal lover have in a relationship with someone who loves country music?"

"I guess I never thought of it."

"I've been thinking about a lot of things lately."

He raises a brow. "Care to share?"

"Are you and I in a relationship?"

His brows meet in the middle. "Of course we are."

"You're not seeing anyone else?"

"I told you before. I'm a one girl at a time kind of guy. That girl is you."

"So, I'm your girlfriend."

He grins, "Yes, if you want to be."

I do believe that is what I want. "Well, then let's get that news out on Facebook. It's not real until it's officially announced there." I have a brief moment of anxiety after I say it out loud.

"Okay, you do that. I'm not good with that social media stuff." He takes something out of the fridge and pops off the lid. "Here."

I smile, looking down at the container of grapes, cheese, and carrot sticks. "You packed *snacks*?"

"Are you making fun of me?"

"Not at all, I think it's kind of cute."

He puts a container of fruit beside me on the table and takes out a box of fish-shaped crackers. "Single dad here. I take snack time seriously."

"Good to know I'll never starve to death."

"Not on my watch."

When the pizza finally arrives, I'm not really hungry anymore. Roger devours several pieces and I wonder where the hell he puts it all.

Picking up the container of strawberries, I move from the hard, uncomfortable chair by the desk and sit on the bed. Roger follows. I open my mouth and take a bite of the large, red, succulent fruit and moan my pleasure. A second bite leaves me holding nothing but the hull. I discard it and lick my fingers. I hear Roger take a strange breath, and as I turn toward him, he snatches the strawberry container out of my hand and practically tosses it onto the table.

He kisses the sweet berry nectar from my lips with a growing passion. I love the way we kiss. My hands caress across his body, firing up every nerve in his muscular body. He reciprocates, exploring until he finds his way beneath my dress. The light brush of his fingertips across the bare skin of my thigh makes me tremble.

Aware of the change in Roger's breathing I pull him closer, encouraging him further. He obliges, the weight of his body forcing me to lie back as he moves to lay on top of me.

His legs tangle with mine, enlivening my desire. I run my fingers through his hair and pull his lips back to mine. Cupping my breast beneath his hand, he squeezes it firmly, making a low feral growling sound. I want him. I need him. I unbutton his shirt and smooth my hands over his chest, exploring the ridges of muscles on an intimate level.

The heat of his breath leaves behind a warm trail as he nibbles his way down my throat. All I can think about is getting out of this dress and pressing his body against mine. Skin on skin. I start to lift it, but he stops me.

"We don't have to go there."

"I know."

He moves to hold my hands, stopping them. "This wasn't my intention."

"I know," I persist, still trying to pull my dress up.

Conflicted, he releases my hands. "Victoria,"

The conscience-stricken look on his face makes me pause. "We're in a committed monogamous relationship, right?"

"Yes."

"I want this." His body presses against me and I know that he wants it, too. I strip off my dress in one quick movement, then reach for the button on his pants. He tenses, the muscles in his stomach tightening when my hand brushes against it. I struggle to try and get them undone. It's been a long time since I've been this nervous about trying to get a man out of his pants. Needing to relieve some of the uncomfortable pressure they're causing, Roger gets to his feet and drops them to the ground, briefs and all. I use the opportunity to rid myself of my undergarments.

He takes a long desirous look at my body before he rejoins me. I don't think anyone has ever looked at me that way before. Emotions well up inside me, threatening to bubble to the surface. When he kisses me, it grows stronger. The sparks...the attraction...the connection. The transfer of energy between bodies makes my heart race. Roger takes his time, getting to know every curve of my body. His lips follow the same path his hands have just taken.

"We don't have to go any further," he whispers, determined to give me an out. "I don't have to have sex to enjoy my time with you. I'm not that kind of a guy."

I ignore him as I smooth my hands over his biceps and upward toward the hard, masculine breadth of his shoulders. My nipples become harder and more sensitive as my chest expands against his. He surrounds one with his mouth, using his tongue to edge me further into arousal. Gentle suction, followed by a firm nip of his teeth, teases me into a quivering, moaning mess. Sliding his hand between my thighs, he gets the confirmation that he's looking for.

His hands follow the contour of my arms and firmly band around my wrists, pulling them above my head and pinning them there. I've never craved someone as much as I do Roger right now. The brief moment that it takes him to move his body on top of me is too long for my liking. I moan loudly when the tip of him rubs across me as he lines up our bodies. My sharp intake of breath, as he enters me, causes him to lengthen and grow harder inside me. That alone almost makes me orgasm on the spot.

With the full weight of his body on me, he remains still, allowing my body to grow accustomed to him. When he tightens the grip on my wrist, and I feel his warm breath exhaled against my neck, I know what's about to come. His first hard thrust makes my body keen. It feels like forever before the next hard slamming of his hips against mine. He releases my wrists, finally allowing me to touch his body. And I do, cherishing every muscle and hard line of it. Supporting himself on strong biceps, he finds his rhythm and quickens his pace.

Waves of pleasure wash over me, building in strength and aching for release. In between panted breaths, Roger claims me with impassioned kisses. I lift my hips, meeting his every thrust, while my hands dig into his dampened skin. Roger slows his pace, almost completely withdrawing between strokes. Supporting himself on muscular biceps, he raises his upper body, as he stares into my eyes and growls. Friction pushes me over the edge of ecstasy, as Roger too, finds his release.

He collapses on top of me, completely spent. His head rests on my shoulder, while his breathing returns to normal.

"Wow," I whisper, trying to catch my own breath.

"I agree." Rolling to the side, he moves the heavy weight of his body off of mine. "I don't want to hurt you," he explains, as he pulls me back into his arms from the side.

I wake several times in the night, still wrapped in his embrace. Every time I open my eyes, I expect to find that he's gone since it's been a long time I've had sex with a man who actually stayed overnight. If I'm being completely honest with myself, I think that it would crush me if that were the case with Roger. He's different from the others. I feel different when I'm with him. I roll to my side, thinking about it way too much. As if he senses my anxiety, Roger closes the small gap my position change has created between us and pulls me back against his chest. Tugging the tangled blankets out from between us, he lifts them and covers me, presses a gentle kiss on my shoulder, and goes back to sleep.

Chapter Twelve

To say that Valentine's Day changed everything is a huge understatement. Only a few weeks ago, I was convinced I was going to spend the rest of my life alone and now Roger Ford has officially swept me off my feet.

I push the hands-free button on my phone and answer his call.

"Where are you? Are you alright?" he asks concerned.

"FUCKING TRAFFIC!"

He chuckles. "Take it easy, there's no rush."

"People won't get out of my way," I growl. This is the reason I'll never move back to Brampton."

I finally pull into his driveway feeling extremely stressed. I suppose it isn't just because of the city driving, I'm a little anxious about tomorrow as well. It's been a few weeks and I've yet to meet his family or any of his friends. Not to mention, I haven't exactly won his daughter over either. I'm not quite sure how she's going to feel about me staying over tonight.

Roger takes my overnight bag out of my hand as I walk through the door. The anxiety is still making me tense. "Almost forty-five minutes to drive a few miles through town!" I complain.

He drops my bag on the floor and it startles me. Grabbing my hand, he pulls me into his arms. "Shh," he whispers. "Listen."

I concentrate on the tune that's playing in the background and smile. "It's your favorite song."

He presses a kiss on my lips. "Forget about everything else right now."

Taking me in hold, he lifts my right hand and bands his arm around me with the other. Then to my surprise, he dances me down the hallway and around the kitchen. Being close to him erases all my angst. I think at one point I giggle at his fancy footwork. As the tension leaves my body, I lean my temple against his jaw. "You've been practicing."

"Nope. It just seems so natural with you."

There's no swaying in the same spot today. He leads me across the kitchen floor with ease and I do my best to follow, giving him a goofy apologetic grin when I mess up. Roger smiles at me adoringly and I really wish I could read his mind. When we run out of room and we're backed against the counter he turns me, and I lock eyes with Molly, watching from the doorway. I stiffen, causing Roger to pause, concerned.

"Hey, Molly." I pull out of his arms. "Do you want to dance with your dad? I heard you're an excellent dancer."

She shakes her head. Her beautiful blue eyes don't hide her melancholy. I can see the pain and hurt reflected there.

"Let's go watch a movie then," Roger suggests.

"What about dinner?"

"I ordered pizza. No pineapple. It should be here soon."

"How many nights in a week do you order pizza?" I ask curiously.

Roger shrugs, looking embarrassed.

I'm sure I don't want to know the answer of that, but the stack of greasy pizza boxes beside the recycle bin is a pretty good indication that it's more than a few times a week. "I'll make popcorn. Do you want to help me, Molly?"

My request is met with silence.

"Molly," Roger prompts.

"No, thank you," she finally responds.

I hold up my hand, stopping Roger from reacting.

"Wish me luck then, I always burn microwave popcorn."

"I'll help," Roger offers.

"Nah, it's okay. You and Molly pick a good movie. I'll figure it out. I've got something special up my sleeve."

"Mmm, burnt mystery popcorn. Can't wait."

"Be nice to me, or I won't share."

"I am being nice," he laughs.

I close the microwave door and double check the instructions on the back of the box before pushing start. I'm unpacking the grocery bag and putting stuff out on the counter, when the loud shrill of the smoke alarm makes me jump.

"Shit!" I pull open the microwave door and wave my hands trying to clear the black smoke. Coughing, I open the small window above the sink and hope it helps. I stick my head around the corner to find Roger standing on a stepladder under the smoke detector. He glances over at me and tries to hold back a smile. "I'll just take the batteries out, until you're finished in the kitchen."

I scrunch up my face, feeling embarrassed. "Sorry."

I disappear back into the kitchen and begin cutting up the fruit I bought and arranging it on a large plate. While I rinse the berries off in the sink, I keep a close eye on the second bag of popcorn. This time, I've got it right. Brilliant blue eyes watch me from the doorway as I pull the bag out of the microwave and try not to burn myself on the steam.

"Molly, I could really use your help here."

She takes a step into the room and stops.

"Do you like M&M's?" I ask as I dump the popcorn into a large bowl. I thank the heavens, when she nods her head. "Can you dump these into the bowl for me while I dry off the berries?" I hold out the bag of chocolate M&M's and wait for her to respond. I'm just about to give up when she takes them out of my hand. Progress.

Molly carries the bowl of popcorn into the other room and I follow behind. With a slice of pizza folded in half and jammed half way into his mouth, Roger watches me place the plate on the coffee table. "You ladies have been hard at work. Is that fruit?" He grabs a piece of watermelon and shoves it into his mouth.

I roll my eyes. "Yes, it comes like this, you know. Not just in rollup form." I move to sit beside him, and I catch Molly's angry stare. Stepping over his feet, I make my way to the chair in the corner.

"Where are you going?"

"I don't want to take Mo's spot. I'll sit over here."

Roger acknowledges Molly's disposition and sighs. He passes me a slice of pizza and makes sure Mo is good to go, then starts the movie. It's been a long time since I've sat through a kids' movie. And I don't think I've ever sat through one geared for little girls. I'm not exactly sure what a *Moana* is but it has Dwayne 'The Rock' Johnson in it, so I'll suffer through it.

Roger raises his one eyebrow, and flexes his pectorals, trying to win me over. It's adorable to watch, but he's not even close. Even animated "The Rock" has got it going on!

When the credits start to roll, Roger lifts Molly off the couch, trying not to wake her. I hear him grunt as he carries her up the stairs to her bedroom.

I clean up the pizza boxes and clear the snacks off the coffee table while I wait for him. In a few short minutes his arms band around me as I stand at the sink washing the dirty dishes. I waste no time in passing him the dishtowel.

"What do you want to do now?" I ask when we're done.

He waggles his eyebrows. "Hot tub?"

"Isn't it kind of cold out?" I stretch to look out the sliding doors in the kitchen.

"The water is one hundred and three degrees," he reasons. "You're going to love it, I promise. We don't have to stay out for long."

He grins from ear to ear when I agree. By the time I get changed into my bathing suit, Roger has removed the cover and poured us both a drink. I open the sliding glass doors and step outside onto the uncovered back porch. He extends his hand and warns me to step safely. Sinking into the bubbling warm water of the Jacuzzi, I forget about the cold Canadian air. Roger turns off the outside lights and slips in beside me.

Now I know why he enjoys this so much. I lean back and let the water surround me. The night sky is so crystal clear I can see every brightly shining star. Roger gives me a boyish smile. Sometimes I worry about what goes on in that mind of his. Before I have a chance to question him about what he's thinking, I have my answer. His hand slides skillfully beneath my bathing suit.

"Seriously?" I ask.

He shrugs, "Why not?"

"Because your neighbors might see us."

Roger looks around the well-sheltered, heavily treed backyard. "I highly doubt it."

He brushes my wet hair off my shoulders. Gathering it in his hand, he uses it to pull me closer to his waiting lips. I'm defenseless when this man kisses me and he knows it. He glides me through the water and onto his lap to meet with a shocking situation.

"Why aren't you wearing pants?" I gasp.

"The real question is, *why are you?*

I look over the edge of the hot tub and find his swim trunks in a pile on the cement stones. "How the? When did you take them off?"

Roger silences me with another kiss while his hands travel my body, sliding my bathing suit bottom down over my hips. The fact that he's so playful and carefree is only one of the things that I love about him. Me? I'm pretty uptight. I become nervous and reach down to stop him.

He nibbles down my neck to my shoulder. I feel my body start to betray me as his hands move to my breasts, pinching and squeezing until my nipples become taut and aroused. As the Jacuzzi lights change from blue to green, all my inhibitions become lost and I lift myself, allowing him to rid me of my bottoms. I feel so...*naughty*. I can't believe that I'm going to do this. "Just the bottoms," I instruct.

You'd think that moving in the water would be easy, but it's not. In fact, trying to move against the bubbling water of the jets is extremely difficult. There's nothing graceful or sexy about the way I maneuver myself to straddle him. My feet float up, and my head goes under the water. I pull myself back up, over the water line, and the top of my bathing suit fills with air. I try to push it down, and it forces out large bubbles that pop loudly to the surface of the water.

"That was not what you think it was," I say, embarrassed when Roger laughs.

Smiling, he grabs hold of my hips and navigates me into position. With my knees, finally firmly in place on the seat on either side, I tease him, hovering. The tip of him rubs against me but I deny him entry. He makes a strange growling sound.

"Was that an *Arrrr*?" I ask amused, caressing my hands across his chest. "Are we playing pirates?"

"If it helps to get you on my cock, then yes."

"Well, in that case, Captain, I request permission to climb aboard the Jolly *Roger*."

"Permission granted." His fingers dig into my waist as I lower myself onto him. The warm, ebullient water washes away my body's natural lubricant making his entry feel rough and dry. It's an odd feeling. Roger slowly helps guide me up and down at first, almost as if he knows. Then it dawns on me. Surely, it's not the first time he's had sex in this hot tub. I try to put that thought out of my mind as quickly as possible.

Moving in the water allows me to be virtually pain-free. I take full advantage it, raising myself almost to the point of withdrawal before burying his shaft deep inside me. Roger grips my ass firmly with each downward movement.

I hold on to the edge of the hot tub, caging Roger beneath me. My breast lands conveniently against his lips and without hesitation he tugs my suit to the side and takes it into his mouth. I can tell by the rise and fall of his chest that he's growing near to his release. I try to increase the pace but in doing so I almost drown him. I try not to laugh as I wipe the water off his face and change my tactics to calm the wake. Roger digs his fingers into my sides and thrusts his hips upwards. I can't see him in the dark shadows, I'm certain he's making that face. The one he always makes when he comes. He pulls me down hard and pumps himself one last time inside me, grunting as he holds me firmly in place.

I let go of my hold and lay against his chest, allowing the warm water to cover my skin. Roger lifts me up as he gets to his feet, making me squeal as he turns and sits me on the edge. Stepping out he holds a towel open in front of me.

"Take it easy," he advises, watching me carefully. I lift one foot over and sit straddled over the edge. That was the easy one, now I have to get the other one over. I cringe slightly as I move the stiff joint over the side, gently slide down to my feet and shiver. "Let's get you in the house."

He follows me into his bedroom, then scoops me off my feet and lowers me to the bed.

"What are you doing?" I giggle as he grabs the edge of the towel and tugs on it, unrolling me.

"Oh, my girl, I'm not finished with you yet."

This time I waggle my brows. "Are we still playing pirate?"

"When I'm done searching for treasure down here, I might let you play with my wooden leg." He joins me on the bed, forcing apart my knees and settling between my legs.

I begin to say something witty but lose my train of thought as he runs his warm wet tongue across me. He teases me with each long lick, making me squirm. Up one side and down the other, circling the giant red X on the treasure map but drawing out the search. I wiggle beneath him, trying to guide him to my clit.

He lifts his head and looks me straight in the eye. I can tell that he's amused. "Mmm. I love deep-sea diving."

I knew he was teasing me on purpose! "Shh," I push the top of his head back down. "Keep searching for the pearl."

I'm sure he just laughed out loud, and I'm about to join him, when he runs his hands across the sensitive nerves down there and parts the seas, uncovering his treasure. I grasp tightly onto the blanket when he surrounds it with his mouth. Roger caresses my thighs, before sliding his hands underneath me. Taking a firm hold of my ass cheeks, he secures me against his face. He appeases me with long licks and the flick of his tongue. I look at the ceiling and whisper a thank you to the higher powers for sending me a man who can breathe through his ears. I'm trapped, unable to move, as he licks, sucks and nibbles. He doesn't quit until my legs begin to tremble and I'm a wet, moaning, mess.

I turn my head, trying to muffle the sound against the blankets when I cry out. Roger doesn't come up for air until the very last ripple of the brilliant orgasm subsides. When he climbs up beside me, he pulls the covers over us as he wraps his arms around me. I snicker as I wipe my hand over his damp beard.

"What?" he asks.

"You look like a glazed donut."

"That's good." He grins and tries to nuzzle against me.

"Eww. Don't! Go wash your face," I demand.

"Nope. I'm going to leave it just like this, so I can smell you all night long while I sleep."

He closes his eyes and it occurs to me that he's completely serious. "That's really kind of sweet. And incredibly disgusting."

"Are you going to go to sleep, or do I need to fuck you again?"

Difficult decision. Who needs sleep?

Chapter Thirteen

I open my eyes and find Ford still wrapped around me like bacon on a scallop. "Good morning," I whisper, sensing that he's awake.

"Good morning, beautiful."

"Are you okay?" I ask, concerned, when he tightens his grip.

"Yeah, I just can't get close enough to you right now."

I know exactly how he feels. I find myself trying to close the space between us on a regular basis. I crave the feeling of his skin against mine. I need the warmth of his body surrounding me. It doesn't matter how close he is to me; I want him closer.

For years I walked alone in this world. People would always argue I might have been alone, but I was loved. And they were right, I was, and I was very blessed for it. But there's a big difference between being loved by your friends and family and being loved by a man.

They're not the same kind of love at all. Well, at least not in my mind.

You can't substitute the caring love of a parent for the soulful intimacy a woman needs from a man. The kind of man who builds her up and keeps her safe. The kind of man who cherishes her on every level and walks beside her...proudly. Everybody needs that from their partner, or they might as well just shrivel up and die, because they aren't really living. I know; I merely existed until Roger's spark brought me to life.

Roger brushes the hair off my shoulder and presses his lips there. "I could get used to this."

"Are you sure you'd want to wake up beside me every morning, Ford?"

"Of course, why not?"

"I'm not always so pretty in the morning."

"You're always beautiful to me," he whispers in my ear.

"Let's see how long that lasts," I snicker.

"Where are you going?" he asks, as I pull myself out of his arms and sit on the side of the bed.

"It's getting late. We're meeting your parents for lunch. Remember?" I grab my socks and begin to get dressed.

"And my sister."

I stop, mid-sock and almost tip over. "Umm. You didn't mention that before."

"I didn't?"

"No."

"Huh. Well, it isn't a big deal. My sister and her fiancé are going to be there, too."

Not a big deal? The man clearly has no clue.

♥

I make a smiley face with chocolate chips on the top of a monster size pancake and put it in front of Molly. She's been giving me the death glare since she came downstairs and found me in the kitchen. Hopefully, it'll warm her up a little.

Roger and I sit across from each other and eat our breakfast while debating over whom the cooler of the two is; Road Runner or Wylie Coyote. Molly uses the prongs of her fork to flick each chocolate chip across the table, one by chocolaty one. We both ignore her at first, but it doesn't stop. I excuse myself from the table to tend to *something*, but I really just wanted to get out of the room so Roger can deal with her behavior, without getting me involved. I'll just politely eavesdrop from the hall.

"I'm not sure what's gotten into you, little girl, but your behavior is unacceptable. You need to apologize to Tori. Clean up the mess, then go upstairs and get ready. We're meeting Gramma and Aunt Jackie for lunch. I'll be up in a minute to help with your hair."

"Is *she* coming?"

My heart sinks in my chest.

"Yes, she is."

"I'm sitting way far away from her at the end of the table," she says angrily.

Hearing her heavy footsteps approaching the hallway, I pretend to be looking for something in my purse. She stops a few feet away and waits for me to acknowledge her.

"I'm sorry I didn't like your stupid chocolate chips," she grunts at me as she stomps up the stairs.

Roger charges out of the kitchen after her and I step in front of him. "Don't. Not now."

"I can't just let it go."

I place my hand on his chest, trying to stall him. "I know, but it can wait until later when you're not so mad. Talk to her then."

He runs his fingers through his hair and growls, "You're right."

I wrap my arms around him and try to erase his frustration. I'm nervous enough today, I don't need him to be all stressed out.

"Daddy!" Molly calls from upstairs. "I need your help!"

His forehead wrinkles and his lips press shut.

"Go," I encourage "I'll finish getting ready down here." While he's busy with Molly, I straighten up around the family room trying to keep busy. The light accumulation of house dust shows signs that there are several objects missing from the room. Judging from the marks left behind I'm going to guess they were most likely pictures that his ex took with her.

I hear Molly enter the room behind me. "We need to teach your daddy how to dust," I say as I spin around. My eyes open wide and my chin drops. The poor girl stands in front of me looking extremely uncomfortable. "Oh," I try to soften my reaction. "Daddy did your hair?"

She nods her head and tears come to her eyes.

"It looks pretty," I lie. "Did you want it in a ponytail?

She nods through the discomfort.

"Would you like me to fix the elastic?"

"Yes, please."

"Let's go back upstairs."

Roger meets us on the landing and gives me an inquisitive look. "What's going on?"

I wait for Molly to get to the top of the stairs. "You pulled the elastic too tight."

"Isn't it supposed to be tight so it doesn't fall out?"

"Yes, but." I stretch my neck to make sure Molly's in her room. "You pulled it so tight you made her look Asian."

"Oh." His shoulders slump. "I don't know how to do these things."

I narrow my eyes. "Did you really use the grocery elastic off the broccoli stem?"

He looks down and away, ashamed. "Maybe."

I put my hand over my mouth to stifle a small laugh. "Go clean out your car, I'll fix it."

Molly is sitting on a chair in front of a child's size, princess vanity, waiting. "Well then. Let's see what we can do." I slowly and cautiously try to remove the twisted elastic from her hair without causing her any further pain.

When I finally get it free and toss it into the garbage, she breathes a sigh of relief.

I dig through my purse. "I think I have something in here. Ah! I do." I put the small package of coated hair elastics on the vanity in front of her. "These are what we need. I'll leave them here for you." I brush the knots out of her hair like an old pro and smile at her in the mirror.

"It hurts when Daddy does it."

"Well, daddies don't know much about brushing the knots out of a girl's hair. You and I have the same curls."

She smiles, and for a very brief moment, I see a sparkle of light in her eyes. Then she glances to a small framed picture on the side of the vanity and her expression dims.

"Is that your mom?"

She nods.

"She's very beautiful. Just like you." I pick up the hair elastic and give it a twist, securing her curls into a beautiful flowing ponytail on top of her head. I need to be just as delicate with this conversation. "You must miss her."

Her lips close tightly, and she shrugs, watching me carefully for my reaction.

Standing behind her, I give her a reassuring smile in the mirror. "It's okay to miss her. SO...now you have pretty hair, are you happy with the outfit Daddy picked out for you?" I swing open the closet door and slide the sweatshirts and leggings to the side. "How about one of these?" I hold two beautiful feminine, frilly dresses out in front of me.

Roger whistles when we meet him at the car. "I wondered what was taking so long." He holds the back door open for her. "You look beautiful, Mo."

His acknowledgement makes her glow. He rounds the hood and beats me to the door. "That's quite the transformation." He opens my door and smiles, looking quite pleased.

"I'll consider it a victory." I give him a kiss before I get in.

"Just wait until I get you home tonight," he says discreetly. "I'll give you a *big* reward."

Molly is quite chatty in the car on the way to the restaurant. Roger keeps looking over at me with a goofy smile.

"How old is Aunt Jackie today, Daddy?"

Roger lowers his brow as he tries to figure it out. "You know what? I have no idea and I'm not going to ask."

I blink my eyes a few times and force my mouth closed. Did I really just hear that?

"What's wrong?"

"Today's your sister's birthday?"

"Yeah."

"And you didn't think you should tell me that?"

"No, why?"

"Because! I would have at least bought a card or something." I shake my head and bite my lip, trying to calm my reaction.

"Sorry." He shrugs. "I didn't think it was important."

I laugh once, completely baffled. "It's the first time I'm meeting your sister, and you don't tell me it's her birthday. What is she going to think when I show up empty-handed?"

"She's gonna think her brother is an asshole. But she already knows that."

It feels like I've done a lot of eye rolling the past couple of days. "Unbelievable, Ford."

Of course, we're a good twenty minutes early for our reservation. Everyone is already waiting inside because, apparently being early is genetic. There's no mistaking mother and daughter; they are both stunningly gorgeous.

Roger suddenly seems nervous as he begins his introductions. "Victoria, this is my mom and dad, Barb and Ted." He pauses, allowing me to shake their outreached hands. The formality of it starts to make me nervous as well. "Well, I can see where Roger gets his good looks." I catch myself staring at his father. They look exactly alike and it's not too shabby if Roger's going to age that well, too.

"And my sister, Jacqueline, and her fiancé, Matt," Roger continues.

"It's really nice to meet you finally. Happy Birthday. I'm sorry, I would have brought you a card, but I didn't know until just now."

She laughs. "That doesn't surprise me."

Roger helps me with my jacket and then holds my chair while I sit. As promised, Molly makes her way to the furthest spot at the end of the table, beside her aunt. I wave at her playfully a few times, but she ignores me. We're barely midway through our meal when the interrogation begins.

"So you live in Orangeville?" Ted asks.

"Yes. I was born in Toronto but moved to Orangeville after I was married. I thought it would be a great place to raise my kids."

"Did Roger tell you he was raised there?"

"Of course I did, Dad." He looks at me apologetically.

"And you work in Mississauga. Is that correct?"

"Yes, I make the commute into the office every day."

"What type of work do you do?"

"Ah, well that's a hard one to answer really. I work for a distribution company. It's not really office or administrative work." I pause for a moment, trying to figure out how to explain it. "My boss normally introduces me as *Special Ops*. I'm the data expert, which is a fancy way of saying that I look after all the regulatory, product, and pricing issues."

"Sounds interesting," his mother adds.

"It keeps me busy. I get assigned to special projects at our other locations, so I travel out of town occasionally."

"Anywhere interesting?" Jackie asks.

"Last time I was sent to Wisconsin to handle an operational crisis. My boss is talking about an issue they're having in California, so I may have to go there next."

"I could handle California," she says. "Are you going with her, Roger?"

His forehead creases. "I don't think so since this is the first time I've heard about it."

"Oh, I'm sorry. He mentioned it yesterday to me, I don't have any details yet."

"And you're annoyed at me for forgetting to mention my sister's birthday?"

I frown. He has a really good point.

"Do you have any siblings?" his mom asks.

"Yes, I have a younger brother."

Roger's head snaps toward me, surprised.

"Poor you," Jackie adds. "Little brothers are a pain in the ass."

"Hey," Roger protests.

"We'll talk later," she promises me.

"Great. I can fuck things up on my own, you know. I don't need your help."

During the course of lunch, his family asks me all matter of questions, trying to acquaint themselves with the *new woman*.

Roger excuses himself to use the restroom, but I know him all too well. He's on his way to intercept the bill. We really are a lot alike.

"You should know," Barb begins once he's out of earshot. "Roger's dad and I are very concerned. We think it's too soon for him to be thinking about another relationship."

"Mind your own business, Mom," Jackie adds from the far end of the table, as she gets up to escort Molly to the restroom.

"I understand your concern. I really do," I assure her. "I know he hasn't been on his own for very long, and there's Molly to consider."

"The wee girl is very fragile."

"I have no intentions of hurting anybody."

"It was a right, cruel thing his ex-wife did to them."

"All he's told me was that she left and doesn't want anything to do with either one of them."

A pained expression washes over her. "Well, you should know, before she left; she made absolutely sure that she made him feel like a complete failure as a man."

I watch him return to the table and my heart starts to feel heavy.

"What's going on?" he asks concerned, looking between us.

I force myself to smile. "Nothing. You paid the bill, didn't you?"

"Hey, I was going to pay the bill," Ted protests.

"It's okay. I got it."

Ted unfolds his wallet and starts to count out bills.

"Put your money away, Dad. I'm not taking it."

Completely ignoring him, he places several bills down in front of him.

Roger pushes the bills back across the table, agitated. "Just let me do this, will ya?"

"Yeah, let him do it, Dad," Jackie adds, putting on her coat.

I get to my feet to say goodbye and she immediately pulls me in for a hug. "It's nice to finally meet you. My brother looks like a very happy man. I haven't seen him smile in a very long time." She releases me and does up her jacket. "We'll do lunch, you and me. We have much to talk to about."

"Absolutely."

"Let me know if you need a travelling companion for California. I'm in."

I smile. I think I'm going to like having a sister.

Chapter Fourteen

I'm not really sure when our lives tangled together so completely that there are rarely any moments we spend apart. Except for the times when Roger works the nightshift. I hate those nights. Every other evening we've gone to bed together at either his home or mine. I love waking up in the morning, safely wrapped in his arms.

Today isn't one of those days. He worked all night and then drove home to get some sleep. I sit at my desk and eat my lunch, having a hard time focusing my thoughts. Pathetic, I know, but I miss him.

The phone startles me out of my funk. "Why are you awake?" I ask concerned.

"The phone woke me up and I can't get back to sleep. I just needed to hear your voice."

"You need your sleep. Close your eyes and dream of me."

"I don't need to dream of you, I have you. Besides, if I think of all the things, I want to do to you, I'll get hard. Then there's no chance of me getting any sleep."

"I wish I was there."

"Me, too. If you thought you were sore yesterday, you just wait until I'm finished with you tomorrow."

"Stop it. I'm at work and I don't have any dry panties with me."

I love that wicked, devilish laugh of his.

"What are your plans for tonight, while I'm slaving away at work all night?"

"It's Wednesday."

"Ah, so you're going dancing."

"Yes, sir. I haven't been in quite a while. Jen's picking me up at seven."

"I'll message you when I get to work. Be safe."

"I always am." I pause for the usual awkward parting words.

"Okay, take care."

"Yup, *take care.*"

♥

A night of line dancing lessons at Nashville North in Norval is one of our favorite things to do to burn off a little steam on a Wednesday night. Of course, Jen is a lot better at it then I'll ever be.

"Every time you talk about him you glow," she comments on the way home in the car.

"That's just sweat. I'm old and line dancing is a lot of work."

"And yet, some of those old girls can dance circles around us both," Jen laughs.

"I know! It's shameful."

"Seriously, though. Things are good? Roger is the man of your dreams?"

"Don't be going all crazy on me now. There are no such things as fairytales."

"Says who?"

I shake my head. "You know, it's only been a few months."

"But more than four dates!"

I roll my eyes. "Yes, more than four dates. We spend a lot of time together."

"That's good!"

"The scary thing about meeting someone online was that they all have polished profiles and pretty pictures. They spin amazing stories of who they are and what they're looking for. Whether it's true or not is an entirely different thing. It was my experience that it was very rarely true."

"That's really sad... and scary."

I nod. "Here's the thing. You can't hide *asshole* forever. Eventually, their true self comes out."

Jen turns the corner and stops in front of my house. "And Roger?"

"I think we're past the point where he's on his best behavior for first impressions. I think he really is the person I've gotten to know. He's a *really* good guy."

"I knew it!" Her celebration ends as her brow lowers in concern. "Are you crying?"

"No."

"Whatever," she teases.

"Roger and his stupid **F**-word."

"**F**-word?"

"**F**eelings," I clarify. "I've cried more in the past eight weeks than I have in the past eight years. I'm an emotional train wreck these days," I laugh, and wipe away my tears.

"Look at you." She throws her arms around me. "I'm so happy for you. And you didn't think you could ever be interested in a *nice* guy."

I smile. "Well, just because he's a nice guy, doesn't mean he doesn't have a bad boy side."

"Oh?"

"Mmhmm, and he's quite the dirty talker."

"Get out!"

I scrunch up my face. "I'm trying to get used to his lack of filter."

"What do you mean?"

"He speaks his mind and doesn't really care who hears."

"Like what?" she asks curiously.

"The other day we were picking up a few groceries and he turns to me in the checkout line and says... *I just want to rip your panties off and lick your pussy right here. I don't even care who's watching.*"

Jen's chin drops, then she bursts into laughter. "I know how uncomfortable that would make you."

"Obviously, that's why you're laughing."

"Obviously," she agrees.

"Most of the time he's the perfect gentleman. You were right, you know."

"Of course, I'm always right," she says confidently. "Wait... what was I right about this time?"

"There's a connection between us. He *gets* me. It's so much more than just physical. When he made love to me the first time, it was like nothing I've ever experienced before."

"Stop it! You're going to make me cry."

I yawn. I don't know how many times I woke up during the night in pain, and I'm fading quickly.

"Thanks for the ride. I'm going to curl up on the couch and have a nap while it's quiet around here. I don't want to go to bed until Roger calls to say goodnight."

Lightning brightens the sky as I rush through the cold pelting rain. As I turn the key, the door flies open hard, pulling the knob out of my hand. It makes me jump. I wander through the dark rooms, trying light switch after light switch but there's no power at all. "Dad!" I call out.

Stumbling into the kitchen, I feel my way to the counter and open the top drawer, looking for the emergency candle and matches that have always been there. Thunder rumbles loudly, making the window shake. "Dad? Where are you?"

I make my way down a long, dark hallway by candlelight. The door at the end seems to be getting further and further away. When I finally get there and reach for the doorknob, everything goes eerily quiet. I look around me at the mysteriously calm surroundings and hold my breath as I push open the door.

"Mom!" Carson yells, shaking me. "Mom, stop screaming it's just a nightmare."

I open my eyes and look at my youngest son. It takes a moment to register what's going on. I force myself to take slower breaths and try to calm down. When I stop trembling, he lets me go.

"I'm sorry, Carson."

"It's okay."

"No, it's not. It's these stupid pain meds. I need to get off them."

"If you let go of my shirt, I'll get back to my game."

I look down to find I've got the bottom of his shirt twisted in a death grip. "Yeah, sorry," I sigh.

He pats me on the head like a small child and heads back upstairs.

I'm just crawling into bed when Roger calls.

"Are you okay?" he asks concerned.

"Yeah, I fell asleep on the couch and had another nightmare. I woke up screaming and scared the crap out of my kid."

"Do you want to tell me what it was about?"

"Not really."

"Okay," he says, sounding displeased.

"I'm just really beat. The meds make me tired."

"I'll talk to you later then. Take care."

I don't know why that always makes me feel so awkward. "Yeah. *Take care*," I mock.

Pure exhaustion ensured my sleep. I don't think I even rolled over once. I stand at the kitchen counter going through my morning routine and get my stuff ready for work. I open my meds and dump the last pill into my hand and glance at the clock on the microwave.

Luckily, the pharmacy is open early so I can pick up my refills on the way to work.

I wait forever in line to get my prescription. Apparently, everyone else in Dufferin County decided to do the same thing.

"That's one hundred and eleven dollars," the clerk advises.

"Holy crap! Is that the full prescription cost?"

"No, ma'am. That's just your portion of the payment. Your medical insurance paid the rest."

I shake the bottle of little white tablets. "Are these things from some remote exotic island and mined by the local indigenous folk?" I hand her my credit card.

"No, ma'am. They're manufactured by Pfizer."

I shake my head. "I was joking."

She looks up at me without a smile. "Your card's been declined."

I stand there completely embarrassed as she attempts to process each of my debit and credit cards, all with the same outcome. I'm broke.

"You can come back," she finally says, growing tired of me scrambling through my purse for change. I can hear the impatient rustling of people behind me.

"Thank you." I stuff my wallet and everything else back in my purse and head to the bank next door to check my account balances. I don't get paid until next week and I only have eighty-three dollars to my name. I've been talking about getting off this medication anyway. Looks like my mind's been made up for me.

♥

"What's going on?"

"I need a big favor."

"Anything for you, Roger."

"I have to put in a few hours of overtime tonight. My sister is staying with Molly for a few hours after school, but she can't stay until I get home."

I hesitate. "Do you think Molly would be okay if I went over?"

"My mom and dad are out of town, I'm desperate."

"Okay, I'm on it."

"Thank you! I owe you."

"Yes, you do."

I put on my sweater and lock my office door. What in the hell have I just gotten myself into?

I find Jackie in the kitchen washing dishes.

"Hey! Reinforcement has arrived."

"I'm so sorry. I'd stay if I could."

"Pfft, no problem at all. Where is she?"

"She's upstairs. We just finished dinner and she's doing her homework."

My eyes get round. "They have homework at that age?"

"That was my thought, too." She hangs the dishtowel on the edge of the counter.

"Jackie, can I ask you a question?"

"Sure."

"How long were you and Matt together before you said *I love you*?"

Her mouth curves into a smile. "I don't remember how long we were dating when it happened, but I'm pretty sure that I was the first one to say it."

"How did you meet?"

"It's a long story." She looks at her watch. "Matthew and I have known each other since we were kids. After graduation, he left the country and I married the boy next door. We didn't get together until a few years ago."

"Really? I'm intrigued."

"The rest of the story will have to wait until we do that lunch. So has my brother told you he loves you?"

"No, not yet."

"But you want him to?"

I sigh. "I'm not sure. It's a big step and I'm not sure how soon is too soon. I just know that it feels natural and I've almost let it slip a few times when I'm saying goodbye."

"What about Roger?"

I smirk. "He just says...*take care.*"

She rolls her eyes. "Doesn't surprise me. Give him time, he won't disappoint you. He might not say it yet, but I can see it in his eyes every time he looks at you."

She extends her arms and gives me a hug. "Tell Molly I said goodbye."

I find Molly sitting in her room, playing on her tablet. "Hi there. How was your day?"

She peeks at me over top of the tablet and says nothing. When I sit beside her on the bed, she turns the screen so I can't see it. "What are you doing? Playing a game?"

"Yes."

"Cool." I glance down at the reminder that just popped up on my phone. I had completely forgotten about the mani/pedi that I booked with the gift cards my kids gave me for my birthday. Looks like I'm getting two manicures instead. "Hey, Molly, have you ever had a manicure?"

She stares at me, confused. "You know, where they make your fingernails all pretty and put nail polish on them?"

She gives her head a small shake. "Well, get your coat, we're going to get our nails done."

I call Roger from the car to let him know we're having a girls' night out. I completely understand the hesitation in his voice. I, myself, am shocked that Mo agreed.

The look on her face when we walk into the spa is priceless. She sits beside me watching my every move. It takes me forever to pick a color, but I finally decide on bright pink. Molly picks the same.

When we get home, Roger is waiting, looking a little anxious. "I was wondering if you girls were ever coming home. Let's get you ready for bed, it's getting late."

Molly stops at the bottom of the stairs and turns. "Goodnight, Victoria."

"Goodnight, Molly. Sweet dreams."

Feeling emotional, I quickly glance at Roger, then look away.

"I'll go tuck her in. Are you staying?"

"I don't think so. I think I might go home."

He gives me a half-smile. "Maybe I'll keep you here and fuck the ass off of ya."

My face turns red. "As tempting as that sounds, I'm not really feeling well."

His brow rises with concern. "What's wrong?"

"I'm just feeling a little rundown. Nothing to worry about. I know if I stay here, I won't be getting any sleep."

"Not normally, if I can help it. But if you're not feeling well, I'll keep my pecker in my pants."

I chuckle. "A noble gesture, but I'm not liking the odds."

I kiss him goodbye. "Go spend some time with Molly. I'll call you when I get home."

Chapter Fifteen

Saturday morning I wake up feeling like death. It started with the cold sweats after I dropped off Molly, and then hit me like a ton of bricks in the night. I haven't mentioned it to Roger, but I haven't eaten in days. Wrapped in my blanket, I head downstairs to try and get something into my stomach before I become anemic. I make it as far as the family room and run out of the energy to go any further. I collapse on the couch and whine, not that anybody cares.

I'm not sure how long I've been sleeping here when I wake to the feel of a cool cloth pressed to my forehead. I must be close to death if one of my kids is concerned enough to look after me. Either that or they're hungry and hovering over my body, waiting for me to pass on so they can divide up the cash in my wallet and order a pizza.

I struggle to force open my heavy eyelids. Rough fingertips sweep the damp hair away from my face and tuck it behind my ear. Now I know for certain, that it's not one of my kids. It takes a few attempts, but I finally flutter open my eyes.

I'm not going to lie, I'm glad to hear his masculine voice. "Hey."

"What are you doing here?" I ask, barely audible.

"I came to check on you. Tanner let me in." Even the filtered sunlight through the blinds hurts my eyes and makes my head pound. "Have you eaten anything today?" He places the back of his hand on my forehead, testing for a fever.

"Ugh. I was heading to the kitchen but didn't make it that far." I struggle to get out from under the blanket and sit up.

"What are you doing?"

"Getting up." I try to get to my feet, but somebody stole the bones out of my legs. "Whoa!" Feeling dizzy, I plop back down.

"Stay put. I brought you some homemade turkey soup, I'll warm it up."

"I really don't feel like eating."

"Tough. You're going to. You have to get your strength back."

I'd argue, but I'm too weak. Proof that he's got a point. While he warms up the soup in the microwave, I look at the Tylenol flu tablets he left beside me and try one more time to get to my feet. Stumbling to the bathroom on the main floor, I gasp at the sight of myself in the mirror.

"Everything okay in there?" he yells from the kitchen.

I curse, trying to pull the brush through my tangled hair. "Uh...yeah. Everything's fine."

When I return to other room, he looks excited. "Soup's ready."

I look down at the spread of warm homemade turkey soup and crackers, juice, and a box of tissues. The expensive kind with the lotion in them. "You brought these?"

He moves stuff around to make room on the coffee table, then sits beside me. "Yeah. I didn't want your nose to get all red and sore." He jumps and holds his arm. "Ouch! Why do you keep pinching me?"

I ignore his question and lift the first spoonful of soup to my mouth, taking a small sip. "Mmmm." If I didn't feel so awful, I'd probably jump him right now. "And who made this homemade soup?"

"I did," he says proudly.

"Impressive." I lift the spoon to my lips for another mouthful and pray that he doesn't question me about my shaking hand.

"Yeah, it was in the freezer. I made it from the remains of the Thanksgiving turkey. The first soup I ever made by myself."

"Good for you."

"I was extremely drunk at the time. I dropped my favorite pepper grinder into the broth and fucked it up for good."

I snicker a little at his confession.

My stomach starts to protest the recent invasion of turkey soup. "You don't have to babysit me all day."

"Yes, I do. I'm the reason you're sick."

That's not true but before I can explain he interrupts me.

"Stop talking and eat."

"You're awfully bossy," I complain.

"Not bossy," he corrects. "I just care."

I sit silently, in a pensive moment. I'm not quite sure how to feel about that. My father was the only man who ever really cared about me. He's gone now and left a huge hole in my heart.

"Victoria?"

I lift my eyes to his. They are such kind eyes, gentle and loving.

"Did I say something wrong?" he asks concerned.

I try to force a small smile, but my eyes betray me. "No, not at all."

"I don't suppose you want to talk about it," he says with a pessimistic tone.

I shake my head, no. I'm not ready to speak the truth out loud. It would be a sad and pitiful recount of all my failings, and I'm not eager to share them with Roger.

He reaches over and takes my hand. Squeezing it, he gives me a sympathetic look. "I've told you before, you can tell me anything. I'm here for you." He puts a pillow on his lap and encourages me to lie down. When I do, he pulls the blanket over me, making sure that I'm warm. The gentle caress of his hands soothes me to sleep.

When I open my eyes, I find myself in my own bed. I rub the spot where my head is aching and discover a strange lump there. There's a note on the night table from Roger saying that he's outside with Tanner and to text him when I'm awake. I grab my phone to look at the time, and I'm shocked that I've slept away half the day.

I wander through the backyard with my jacket over my pajamas and wearing someone's size twelve snow boots. They're so heavy I'm not sure where I find the strength to lift my feet. I can hear the boys talking in the driveway, and I stop where they can't see me so I can watch them together. At the moment, they're both bent over the hood of Tanner's car.

"Gentle," I hear Roger say. "You've got to treat her like a woman. Take her slow and easy. It ain't polite to just force it in. There you go. Nice. Now try to fire her up."

I step around the side of the shed, as Tanner climbs in behind the wheel and cranks the engine. It starts right away and purrs like a kitten. Excited, he jumps out of the driver's seat and gives Roger a fist bump. I can't remember the last time I saw the boy look so happy.

"Hey, it sounds like she's running great now."

Roger turns to look at me, shocked. "What the hell are you doing out here?"

"I needed some fresh air and I wanted to see what you two were up to."

Tanner slams down the hood, making me jump.

"How are you feeling?" Roger asks concerned.

"Like I've been hit by a truck."

"Did you take the cold and flu medication I brought?"

"Ummm. No."

"Why not?" He asks annoyed.

I hesitate. I really don't want to tell him why, but I can't lie to him.

"Because they aren't going to help."

"Why not?" he repeats.

Ugh. I've gotten to know Roger well enough to know that this isn't going to go over well. I scrunch up my face and stall.

"Are you going to tell me, or what?"

"They won't work because I don't have the flu." I look away from his icy stare, pretending that I'm watching Tanner pack up his tools. "I stopped taking the nerve blockers. I think I'm going through withdrawal."

"Victoria!" he says sternly. "You can't just stop taking that kind of medication cold turkey. You have to reduce the dosage and ease off of it."

"I know that, now. The side effects were so bad that it seemed like a good idea at the time."

He thinks about it a moment, then shakes his head. "Okay, then." He leans back against Tanner's car and crosses his legs at the ankle. "You tell me how I express that I'm not happy about your decision, without sounding like an asshole."

I stutter, trying to come up with an answer, but I can't. Roger grows impatient. "How bad is it? Do I need to take you to the hospital?"

"No!" I hate hospitals and he knows this. "I'm fine. I can cope."

"You're going to lie to me anyway," he says, aggravated.

I hear Tanner snicker as he rounds the hood of the car, and I flash him an unimpressed look.

"Understand this," Roger continues, "if I think you need to go, you're going to go. I don't care if I have to pick you up and carry you in. You can't fuck around with stuff like this."

I knew he was going to be upset with me. "Roger..."

"Stop. No excuses. I can't lose you; it would kill me."

I feel horrible. I didn't expect him to be this upset. I step forward, moving closer to him, waiting for a response. He sighs and opens his arms, welcoming me. It's a tremendous relief when I snuggle against his chest and he holds me tight.

As I nuzzle in under his chin, I flinch when I hit that tender spot on my forehead. "Did you carry me to bed?"

Roger releases me and gently brushes my hair back, so he can see the lump. "Yeah, I'm really sorry." He cringes. "I misjudged the width of the doorway."

I laugh a little. "It's okay. I'm surprised you could carry my fat ass up the stairs at all. I really need to hit the gym."

"Oh, stop it. I know that you're uncomfortable with your weight, but I really don't like when you say things like that. I won't ever put you down. I love your body. Every inch of it."

"I need to lose twenty pounds," I complain.

"You don't have to change anything for this guy."

Roger is no longer accepting of my inability to fully comprehend and accept the words that come out of his mouth. "I really care for you. Are you getting that yet?"

"Yes." I quickly dab at the corner of my eye, erasing the tear there. "I care for you, too."

"Good." He smiles. "How are you feeling right now?"

"I'm okay, my muscles just feel a little weak."

"Are you up for a drive?"

"Sure." The sun is shining brightly on this unusually mild April day in Dufferin County. It's a perfect day for a drive.

"Great. You get dressed while I help Tanner clean up." He picks up a rag and tries to wipe the grease off his hands.

"Oh, and Victoria..." he calls out to me as I make my way into the house. "Monday morning, you're going to call the doctor and get in right away to get that medication thing sorted out."

♥

"Where are we going?" We've already established several times that I hate surprises.

"Just relax. I want to take you somewhere today."

I tense at his suggestion and he reaches across the console and places his hand on mine.

"I know it's not easy for you but trust me."

I watch the landscape out of the window and try to read street signs, hoping for a clue. It's the last turn that makes me suspicious. We're heading straight out of town.

"Does it matter where we're going?" He squeezes my hand. "It's a beautiful day for a drive and I enjoy your company."

Glancing over at him, I nod my acknowledgement and smile. A few miles of music and pleasant conversation relax me. He makes a turn onto a gravel road and I immediately know where I am. I look at him for confirmation, but he stares straight ahead, pretending that he doesn't know I'm looking at him. When he pulls off onto the grassy shoulder and parks, I stare out the window at the century-old church and the surrounding cemetery.

"My dad is buried here." Becoming a little anxious, my hands fidget in my lap.

"I know. Tanner told me." He gets out of the car and opens my door, holding out his hand to help me.

"Why are we here?" I ask, getting to my feet.

"You've been talking about him a lot lately. I know you've been missing him. I thought it was time for he and I to meet."

I swallow the lump in my throat and try to settle the emotional uprising brewing inside me. Roger reaches over and takes a hold of my hand, keeping me steady as I walk up the grassy hillside, avoiding the patches of mud.

"This is where my grandparents are buried." I stop in front of the large marble tombstone, pausing to read it. "My grandmother said she wanted to be buried side by side so she could reach over and hold his hand."

"That's really romantic."

"Yeah, it is. Odd though, because when he was alive she was always threatening to strangle him."

I hold my breath and take a step to the grave on the right. I drag my foot back and forth over the long grass trying to uncover something. "This is my dad." I frown, looking at the small stone tile. "My mom couldn't afford a tombstone. So this..." I brush the dirt off the small, four-inch, square tile and uncover his initials and the date. "This is all that marks his grave." I try to hold back the tears.

"It's okay. Let it out," he says, trying to assure me that my emotional response is warranted.

I shake my head. "It really bothers me. I've tried to save enough money to buy one myself, but there's always something breaking down around that stupid house."

"Are tombstones expensive?"

"Yeah, disgustingly expensive. But, still... he deserves one. I guess it's one of the reasons I've stopped coming to see him. It really upsets me. He deserves better."

Roger smoothes his hand on my back, trying to settle me. "Sweetheart. Believe me, he would understand."

"You're probably right. Dad always said that life threw him so many curve balls that the only thing he was going to leave me when he died was his debt." I laugh once. "He wasn't kidding." I stand for a long time in silence. He doesn't rush me, nor does he pry. He waits patiently, allowing me to work out whatever I need to work out today. "One of my favorite memories of my dad is when I was a young girl. He used to be a plumbing salesman and a lot of his customers were up north toward the town of Bracebridge. Sometimes, in the summertime, once school was out, he would let me go with him for the day. It always turned out to be a warm, sunny journey through the northern Ontario countryside. I loved the drive through the area where the surrounding rocky terrain was blasted to accommodate the road. I always thought it was really cool that I could still see the drill marks in the rock."

Roger gently brushes my windswept hair away out of my eyes. "I know the area you're talking about. It's a beautiful drive through there."

"Yeah." I pause a moment, mulling over my recollection. "He would pull off onto the shoulder and we'd climb the rocks to pick wild blueberries that were hidden within the heavily treed areas. Sometimes, he'd forget to bring a container to put them in, so we'd sit on the rocks and eat as many as we could." My emotions begin to bubble to the surface, but I still manage to giggle. "Then he'd tell me that we'd better get going before we were eaten by bears."

Roger laughs and passes me a tissue that he's dug out of his pocket.

"You know," I sniffle and wipe my nose, trying to hold off a complete meltdown. "It wasn't until years later that I realized that he must have spent hours looking for those spots on his own, so he knew exactly where to stop when we were together."

He nods his head and hands me another tissue. "You're probably right."

"He would have done anything for me. He would have done anything for my boys."

"Tanner was talking about him while we were working on his car. He seemed really close to him. He said he drives out here sometimes, on his own, when he's missing him."

I wipe away the tears. "When he died, Tanner sat at my kitchen table for two straight days and didn't say a word to anyone."

"How did he die?"

I struggle with the answer. Still battling between wanting to share with him and the need to protect myself.

"Victoria," he whispers, "It's okay to talk about it now. I'm here."

"Tanner called me at work to tell me that my dad didn't pick the boys up from school. I called and I called but I got no answer. My mom didn't have her cell phone turned on. I finally left work and picked up the boys and drove over there."

"You found him." Roger acknowledges sympathetically, as he takes a seat on a dry patch of grass and motions for me to sit beside him.

"It was getting late, and the house was dark. There was a storm and the power kept going out. I found him in his bedroom. He was completely dressed, laying on the top of the covers." I shudder slightly as I think about the part that haunts me in my sleep. "His eyes were wide open. Like he was waiting for me."

Roger puts his arm around me and pulls me to his shoulder. My heart feels so heavy that it hurts, but I can't stop now. I take a stuttered breath and continue, "I didn't know what to do. I called 911. They told me someone was on the way but instructed me to do CPR until they got there. I tried to tell them that he was dead already, but they insisted. I panicked and put my phone on speaker so I could follow their instructions."

Roger holds me tighter as I let out a few sobs. I pull away to wipe my tears and blow my nose. He stares at me, and I can tell by his eyes that he's feeling brokenhearted for me.

"I did what they asked. I pushed on his chest but his body was stiff. They told me to breathe air into his lungs, and I did, but his lips were cold. I knew...I knew that he had been dead for a long time."

"It's okay," Roger assures me, squeezing me tighter. "Let it all out."

My lip begins to quiver and I begin to unravel. I shake my head trying to stay it off. "I'm crouched over my father's cold dead body, while the emergency operator is telling me to place my mouth over his and give him air again, and I just can't bring myself to do it. I look up to see the boys watching from the doorway, crying. Tanner did his best to hold it together and comfort his brothers." I break down into a hard sob. "They stood there, staring at me. I can still remember the look on their faces. It was like..." I stutter, "Like they were thinking that I drove their father away, and now I was taking their grandfather away from them, too."

"Oh, baby, I'm so sorry." He rocks me until I don't think I can cry anymore.

"I always wonder if I just kept doing CPR like they told me to, maybe I could have revived him."

"Sweetheart, no. He was obviously long past the point of being revived. You know that, right?"

"Yes, but..."

"You couldn't have saved him," he insists. "Did you ever find out the cause of death?"

"I spoke with the coroner after the autopsy. He said it appeared to him that his organs just stopped working. That it was his time to die. He said he probably got up and got dressed and started not feeling so well, so he laid down and peacefully passed."

Roger loosens his grip and allows me to pull myself together. I can tell from the look on his face, he has one more question and he's not sure if he should ask.

"What?"

"Where was your mother?"

I frown. "I thought she was out shopping or running errands that day."

"But she wasn't?"

"I found out months later that she was out with another man."

Roger looks deflated. "The high school sweetheart that she's married to now."

"Yes." I get to my feet and wipe the dirt off my bottom. "Maybe, if she was home, she could have saved him. Maybe she could have gotten him help in time."

"I guess that's why you don't talk to your mom often. I'm really sorry."

The sun shines through the trees, warming my face. "Thank you, for bringing me here."

Getting to his feet, he wraps his arms around me and squeezes tightly. "You're welcome. I have nothing else to do today but be here for you. Take as long as you need."

I take a few breaths and get control of my emotions. "I'm ready to go." I pull myself out of his embrace and stuff the damp tissue into my pocket so that I can take his hand.

"Give me a minute, would ya?" He drops my hand and pauses.

I search his eyes, wondering what's behind the look on his face. "Why?"

"I need to have a word with your dad." Roger steps onto the grave and looks down at the small stone marker. "Hi," he begins. "I didn't get the chance to meet you, but from what Victoria has told me, I think I would have liked you."

I stand a few feet behind him, waiting curiously. He clears his throat and shifts his weight from side to side as if he's just had a sudden onset of nerves. Instinctively, I move to his side and reach down to hold his hand.

"You need to know that I love your daughter."

As our fingers interlock together, I feel a very powerful connection between us. My heart pounds.

"I wanted to tell you, I'm very sorry it took me so long to find her."

The breeze picks up and I close my eyes, concentrating on the sound of his voice. A single tear escapes and gently rolls down my cheek. He wipes it away with the pad of his thumb.

"But I promise you, sir. I'll never let anybody hurt her again." He pauses, staying off his own emotional response. "I'm going to take care of her from now on."

I open my eyes and look up at him with an expression of adoration.

"Well," he adds, briefly pressing his lips to my forehead. "That's if she'll let me. You know how stubborn she can be."

"Hey!" I step back in protest and cross my arms.

He smirks. "Well, it's true. Your dad knows that."

I laugh because it's true. I tug gently on his hand and begin heading back to the car.

"Don't think that I didn't catch the L word, just now."

Roger smirks. "Mmhmm. Obviously, you're emotionally exhausted right now, but how does the rest of you feel?"

"I feel fine. Why?"

"I'm going to take you home and fuck you until you *believe* that I love you."

"Roger!" I gasp. "I can't believe you just said that!"

He looks at me horrified. "Oh, no. Was that inappropriate?"

"Yes!" I can't help myself and I start to laugh. "It's the first time you've used that word. That's kind of a special thing."

"Oh," he says with regret.

"And my father is right there."

"I'm sorry!" he yells over his shoulder as we walk. "I respect your daughter."

"OMG! Just get in the car, Ford."

Chapter Sixteen

The heavy spring rain is relentless today. Roger waits for me in the car while I talk to the doctor. On the way to the pharmacy, to pick up a new medication, I can't help but feel like something's a little off. Usually, by now, he would have made at least one inappropriate sexual comment.

"We need to stop for gas."

"I'll get it," I offer as he pulls up to the pump.

"Don't be ridiculous. You'll get drenched."

Ignoring him, I get out and pull up the hood on my jacket.

Roger gets out of the car and steps up behind me, pressing his body against mine. "You can be stubborn." He wraps his coat around me, blocking the wind. "But I'll always win." He reaches down and places his hand over mine and squeezes the trigger. My body responds, heating us both.

I give up on the argument over who's going to pay. I get back into the passenger seat and wait for him to return. Something is definitely bothering him. I sensed it in his body just now. It's a long slow drive to Orangeville, in and out of the rain all the way. When we pull into the lane at the back of my house, the sky opens up. We sit in complete silence waiting for a break in the torrential rain.

The silence is killing me. "Are you upset with me for not mentioning that I might have to go out of town for work?"

He scratches his head, and then tugs at his ear.

"Roger? Talk to me. Something's bugging you."

"Do you think things are moving too fast between us?"

I get a sick feeling in the pit of my stomach. "I've felt that way a few times, yes."

"All day long, I've been trying to figure out how I didn't know you had a brother."

"Oh." I see his point. "I guess it never came up."

"Having siblings isn't something you forget to mention. We're not just getting to know each other here. We're already well established in a serious relationship."

"He left home a long time ago. I haven't seen or heard from him since I was eighteen. I have no idea where he is, what he's doing, or even if he's still alive. I guess in my mind I don't have a brother anymore."

His jaw tightens and I can tell that he's having some sort of internal struggle. I focus my attention on the sound of the driving rain against the windshield and wait it out. I'm not prepared for what comes next. He curls his fingers around the steering wheel and grips it tightly.

"Who is James Baker?"

It feels like I've just been winded by a hard shot to the gut. He turns to look at me when he hears my sharp intake of breath, trying to fill my lungs back with air.

"He was a friend of mine."

He gives me a long slow nod, but I'm certain he doesn't believe me. "Seems like he was more than a friend."

"You've been stalking me on Facebook."

"After finding out that you had a brother, I got wondering what else I didn't know."

"So you've seen his posts and comments."

"Yes, all of them."

I sigh heavily. This is not good.

"Were you dating?"

"Yes..." I shake my head and correct myself. "No. James and I met on Facebook through a mutual friend. It started off with a little flirting on posts."

"I've read some of those posts, Tori. That was not just flirting."

I raise my hands, trying to stop him from getting riled up. "Hold on, you need to know that this was just an online thing. James Baker lives in Texas. We've never met and we'll never meet."

"It looked like it was pretty serious."

"I'll admit I didn't mind the attention. I was pretty lonely and his friendship made me feel *wanted*."

He turns his gaze away from me and the muscle in his jaw begins to tic. "Some of those posts suggested that you and he had a physical relationship."

"Oh." My face begins to flush. "That was his idea. I started having problems with men, who were getting a little out of line. James thought if we portrayed ourselves to be in a relationship that it might deter them. He called it cowboy security."

"Did you have feelings for each other?"

"I suppose we did. Although our entire relationship was *just pretend*."

"Where is he now?"

"No idea. I haven't had any contact with James Baker for over a year." I open my phone and scroll to the last message I received from him. I hand it to Roger to read.

Midnight, Christmas before last. *"I'll always love you."* I scroll down on the screen to show him that's the last message received. "Then he magically disappeared. Deleted his profile or just blocked me." My hands fidget in my lap. "I don't know which one, and I never bothered to investigate any further. Either way, I'm guessing he moved on to something better."

Roger's face remains stoic, surveying my reaction. "If it was just a pretend relationship, then why are you so upset right now? Do you still have feelings for him?"

I fight to stop the tears. "Baker and I were *an online couple* for two years. We were never physically together, but he was a real person on the other side of the screen. I trusted him with my secrets and my fears. He promised me that he would never leave me. I woke up one morning to find that, like all the others, he just...*threw me away*." I reach for the door handle, raining or not, I need an escape.

Roger grabs my arm, stopping me. When I turn to meet his eyes, his body softens. "I'm sorry that all the men in your past have hurt you."

Not knowing what else to say, I shrug.

Roger lifts my hand to his mouth and kisses it, then holds it to his cheek. "I know there's nothing I can do to make you believe me, but I'm not going anywhere. So I guess, I'll just have to prove it to you."

"The rain has stopped. We should make a run for it before it starts again."

We almost make it in time, but the universe is determined to keep us soggy today. It's a damn good thing I'm not made out of sugar. I push open the door, stop at the top of the steps and turn toward Roger, shocked.

"What?" he asks as he joins me. I watch as his eyes widen. "Well, well. Now, who's caught in the act?" We wait, but there's no break in the action. It's as if they don't have any clue that we're in the room so Roger clears his throat. It startles the pretty young blonde, who quickly pulls down her T-shirt and gets to her feet.

"Hi." I enter the room slowly, looking away awkwardly as Dallas gets to his feet and indiscreetly adjusts himself. Roger tries to hold in his amusement, but I hear him snicker. A sharp elbow to the chest should help with that.

My eyes are immediately drawn to the glowing red hickey on her neck. I can't stop staring at it.

"Dallas, could you introduce us to your friend?" Roger prompts.

"Oh, yeah. This is Lindsay."

"Hi, Lindsay. I'm Victoria, Dallas' mom." I'd extend my hand, but the poor girl has her arms crossed in front of her, trying to hide the fact that her bra is laying on the living room floor a few feet away. Lord, could this be any more uncomfortable?

"That's Roger," Dallas points out. "He's my mom's fuck buddy."

I gasp loudly. Apparently, it can get a LOT more uncomfortable.

"Nice to meet you." Roger flashes Dallas a disapproving look, then smiles. "What Dallas meant to say is that I'm his mother's boyfriend."

"Yeah, whatever." He shrugs. "We're going upstairs."

Roger settles on the couch and puts on the TV. I stiffly sit on the edge, still traumatized.

"Are you okay?" Roger teases.

I look at him, astonished. "I had no idea that he had a girlfriend."

Heavy footsteps bound down the stairs. Dallas stops at the doorway and looks between us.

"Don't look now, Mother." Roger teases. "Your boy is in love." As if he knows the reason for his reappearance Roger scoops up Victoria's *not so* Secret and tosses it to him.

Some strange male bonding thing just happened, I'm sure of it. At any moment, I expect them both to start jumping up and down, beating on their chests.

"Right, L O V E. I saw it on her neck," I say sarcastically.

"I had to mark my territory!" he says defensively. "Did you see Lindsay?" Roger snickers when Dallas uses his hands to demonstrate the size of her breasts. This time he's ready for me and dodges the elbow to his chest.

"She's definitely a twelve on a scale of ten," Roger agrees. "But that's not the way to mark your territory, Bud."

"It's not?"

"Nope. It's really very simple. Do nice things for her. Listen when she talks. Cherish her and make her feel like she's wanted. Most women just want to be appreciated, and if you treat them right, they're never going to stray. They'll make sure every man that comes sniffing around knows she belongs to you."

Dallas turns his attention toward me. "Is that true?"

"Well, he's still around, so he must know what he's talking about."

Dallas nods. "Thanks, I guess you're not such a dick after all."

I sigh, "And we were doing so well." Dallas begins up the stairs and my *mother brain* kicks in. "There's condoms in the bathroom cabinet. Use them! I'm too young to be a grandmother."

Embarrassed, Dallas scrunches up his face. "Ew, that's disturbing. How about you don't say that to me ever again."

He stomps up the stairs and slams the door. I look to Roger.

"Really?" he asks amusedly. "Nice timing."

"I don't know how to handle this stuff," I complain. "I'm afraid I'm going to mess things up and ruin the rest of their lives."

"You're being a little dramatic, Tori. One embarrassing moment isn't going to ruin his life. Besides, I think you're more traumatized than he is."

"You're probably right." I loosen up and lean against his shoulder.

"What's the worst date experience you've ever had?"

I don't even need to give that question any thought. "Goggles."

"Excuse me?"

"I went out with a man a few years ago. Nice guy, a few years older than myself." Roger sits patiently, following along. "Things started to progress and one night we were fooling around and, well...one thing led to another." I pause and shudder.

"And?"

"I unzipped his pants with the intentions of rocking his world with the best blow job he'd ever had. When he dropped them to the floor, I damn near had a heart attack."

"Largest dick you've ever seen?"

"No. The largest bush of pubic hair I've ever seen."

"You're kidding me?"

"I kid you not. And there wasn't just a lot of it; it was wild and wirey! Like a tumbleweed."

Roger laughs.

"It's not funny! It took both hands to part that shit and pat it down far enough so I could get to his Johnson. All I kept thinking was I should have worn safety glasses. I COULD HAVE SCRATCHED A CORNEA!"

I've never seen Roger laugh this hard. He holds his stomach and gasps for air.

"I mean seriously, he never thought to look after the manscaping?"

He stops laughing and raises a brow. "Manscaping?"

"Yeah. You know?" I point to his crotch. "Tidy stuff up down there."

"Guys do that?" he asks shocked.

"Guys who want their dicks sucked on a regular basis, do."

The sound of footsteps halts our conversation. "What's so funny?" Dallas asks when he gets to the bottom of the stairs.

I try to look innocent. "Nothing."

He looks back and forth between us and rolls his eyes. "You two are weird. Lindsay is leaving now."

"It was nice to meet you. Mrs. Campbell," she says politely as she puts on her shoes.

"Hey, Bud," Roger says on the sly. "Walk her home. Make sure she's safe." He hands him an umbrella. "Give her a reason to keep you around."

♥

I watch as Roger folds his jeans and tosses them on the stool at the end of the bed. He looks at me strangely as he pulls back the covers he climbs in beside me. "What are you thinking?"

"I'm thinking how amazing and patient you are with my kids."

"They're good kids. I don't think Carson likes me."

I laugh once. "Don't sweat it. Carson doesn't even like me."

"How would you feel about having more?"

"You mean like stepkids?"

He pulls me into his arms. "No."

I raise my eyebrows. "Are you serious?"

"I didn't think I'd want anymore but..." His chest expands. "I love you, and I know it probably wouldn't happen at our age, but I really want to make babies with you. Does that sound weird?"

"I'm pretty sure that when I filled out the section that said 'wants kids' on my dating profile I answered HELL NO."

"I'm just being goofy, I guess."

I brush my fingertips across his cheeks. "Not at all. I actually understand exactly how you feel. I think when you love someone, it's a natural instinct to want to have a family together. A lot of people I know had kids with their new partners. I didn't understand why they'd want more kids at their age, but I get it now."

"Do you think we're too old?"

"I don't know. Sometimes I think those days are past, then I find myself thinking about having another baby."

"I wish I'd met you ten years ago." He holds me tighter.

"I can't even imagine that. The way you like to fuck, we'd probably have a ton of kids by now."

Chapter Seventeen

It's very unusual for Roger to have a restless night. Normally, all he has to do is get a firm hold of my boobs and he's sawing logs in minutes. I lose track of how many times he wakes me up tossing and turning. After several hours of interrupted sleep, he snuggles up behind me and assumes his usual position. I turn in his arms and brush my fingers across his cheek.

"Are you okay? What's going on?"

He rakes his fingers through my hair and thinks on it. "I want to make love to you, so you'll never forget that you're mine."

Ah, I know what this is about. He's still thinking about James. The rising sun lightens the shadows so I can see his face. I trace the outline of his lips with the tip of my finger. "I'm yours." Taking his hand, I place it on my chest. "Your heart and your soul. I think I've always been yours. I've just been waiting for you to find me."

His lips find me *waiting* hungrily for his kiss. With a passion that only Roger can ignite, he sates my desire, breaking away only to whisper those three words that I've been longing to hear. "I love you."

For the first time in my life, I feel safe. I feel loved. His strong, rough hands travel my body, setting every nerve on fire with his touch. When our legs tangle together, and our souls melt into one, Roger Ford makes love to me so deeply and passionately that I'm forever branded as his. No other man could claim me.

In the afterglow of our love, he lay beside me, strengthening our bond and drifting into sleep. When I open my eyes, his arms are wrapped around me and his hands are in their usual spot. "How was that for an early morning romp?" he whispers in my ear.

I laugh, amazed that I have the energy to breathe. Roger presses his hips against my backside, poking himself into me. "Why don't you make this thing hard so I can pound you again?"

I look at him over my shoulder, shocked. "Really? You could go again, so soon?"

He shrugs. "I don't know, but you can try. If it gets hard it's a bone-us."

"That's a horrible joke," I groan

"I don't care about coming. I just want to be inside you right now." He throws the covers off and begins to climb over me. "But first I have to take a leak."

"Now there's a romantic segue."

When he returns to the room, I'm sitting on the side of the bed with my phone in my hand. The look in my eyes makes him pause.

"Who was on the phone?"

"My boss."

Roger's expression dulls.

Guilt makes me look away. "I have to go to California."

"Okay. When?" He moves to stand in front of me and forces my chin up.

I frown. "On the next available flight."

"Today?" his tone escalates. "Are you kidding me?"

"Sorry. You can come with me."

Roger pulls up his jeans and fastens them. "I can't take off with such short notice, Victoria. Even if I could get a few days off work, what do I do with Molly?"

"You're right. I understand. I just didn't want you to think that I'm trying to get away from you. I'd love for you to go with me." I pull my carry-on bag from the top of the closet and begin to fill it, while Roger stands watching. "How long will you be gone?"

"Ten days, or until the crisis is over." I stuff underwear around the edges of the case, filling in all the spaces. Roger disappears downstairs, leaving me to finish packing.

I love the challenges of working on the crisis team. It keeps my mind engaged and stops me from getting bored. I'm lucky that I can do the travelling now that the boys are old enough to look after themselves. I'm pretty sure they look forward to the times I'm out of town. It's a win/win situation for all. Now I'm dreading it.

I half-carry, half-drag my luggage down the stairs, cursing as I bang it off the walls.

"What are ya doing?" Roger says annoyed as he takes the larger of the two bags out of my hand. "Why didn't you call me?"

"I'm used to doing stuff like this on my own."

He flashes me a look and shakes his head. "Well, you don't have to anymore. RIGHT? You have me to help."

I hate it when he says stuff like that. In admitting it, I'm afraid that I'm becoming too dependent on him. Too needy. Something I'd prefer to avoid.

He piles my luggage by the front door and pulls me into his arms, squeezing tightly. "Did you mean it when you said you want me to go with you?"

"I lean back to look at his face."

"Of course."

His whole face lights up. "We have to stop by my house on the way to the airport and grab some stuff. I'm going with you."

"Are you serious?"

"I am. But I can only stay a few days, then I have to come back home. If you weren't serious about me going, tell me now."

"I want you to go!" I say excitedly. "But what about Molly?"

"She's going to stay with my sister."

"I love your sister," I squeal as I throw my arms around him.

"Yeah, she's okay. We'll have to bring her back something nice. She's specifically requested something blond and bronzed. I have no fucking clue what that means."

♥

Roger runs into the house and grabs a bag from the basement. Throwing it onto the bed, he runs around the room, tossing stuff in the general direction. Molly and I ensure it makes it into his suitcase.

Jackie arrives at the same time as the cab. Molly looks up at her dad and waits. Flustered, he isn't thinking straight. "Roger," I prompt.

"Oh," he says looking down. "I'm only going to be gone a couple of days, Mo. You and Aunt Jackie have fun." He crouches to her level and pulls her in for a tight squeeze. The cab driver honks the horn, impatiently.

"Get out of here, would you?" Jackie says, placing her hand on his back.

I pick up the bag that he's left behind and follow him outside. I turn, thinking that I haven't closed the door properly. Molly stands behind me, on the porch. "Is everything okay?"

She nods and throws her arms around my legs. I rake my fingers through her curls and try to get a grip on my emotions. I look over at Roger and there are tears in his eyes.

"Don't worry," I assure her. "Daddy will call you every day and before you know it, he'll be home."

"Are you coming home?"

I think my heart just shattered. "Yes, of course. I have to stay a little longer than your dad, but I'll be back as soon as I can. Aunt Jackie has our phone numbers so you can call anytime you're missing us."

She backs up a few steps and reaches up to hold Jackie's hand. She waves as the cab reverses out of the driveway. Roger reaches over and gives my hand a squeeze. "I swear, Ford. If you make me cry, I'm going to punch you right in the junk."

Anxiety hits him hard in the chest when we check in and he realizes that buying his ticket at the last minute means we aren't seated together. I've never seen Roger look like he's about to come completely undone. Charm and a little flirting convince the gentleman sitting next to me to trade him seats. "You can't miss him," I joke. "He's the guy a few rows up, who looks like he's going to freak the fuck out."

I lean so I can see up the narrow aisle, waiting for him to join me. He hurries to sit down beside me and buckle his seat belt. "I didn't know you were afraid of flying." I try to settle him, but he grips my hand firmly as we taxi out onto the runway. We're a few minutes into the flight when my hand starts to tingle. Needing to restore blood flow to my fingers, I attempt to break free from his grip. He looks at me, feeling embarrassed as I shake my hand.

"It's okay," I assure him. "You'll get used to it. I used to get really nervous when I first started flying."

"You know what would help me?"

"What?"

"A distraction."

"Oh, like watching a movie? Or playing tic-tac-toe?"

"No, like sex."

I grin. "Yeah, sorry, Ace, but that's not happening. You'll understand why when you see the bathroom."

"Fine, I'll watch a movie then."

I hand him the headphones. "Good choice."

I'm thankful it's a smooth, uneventful flight, and before we know it, we're landing in San Diego.

I get a kick out of watching his face as he takes in the beautiful Southern California scenery along the 15 highway.

"We're here!" I pull into the valet out front of the Cape Rey Hilton, just outside of Carlsbad. "I think you're going to like it."

"Oh? Why's that?"

"The ocean is literally right across the street."

Roger walks through the lobby of the prestigious hotel, completely awestruck. "You can afford to stay here?"

"Only because of the corporate rates," I laugh. "Otherwise, not in a million years."

On the way to our room, we pass the beautiful, outdoor swimming pool complete with patio bar that overlooks the ocean. "I think you're right. I'm going to love it here."

"In all the times I've travelled here, I've never been over to see the ocean. I've always been too busy with work."

"We're going to change that."

♥

My first day at the California office is exhausting. There's so much data to review before I can even think about developing a solution. Before I know it, it's after five p.m. Roger has sent several messages, asking what time I'll be back to the hotel, but my phone was on silent. I'm a little nervous about the reception I'll get when I get there.

"I wondered if you were still alive," he says when I open the hotel room door. "Did you lose your phone?"

"No. I just lost track of time." I watch him nervously as he crosses the floor. I try not to wince when he raises his hands, but it's a reflex. When I open my eyes there's no anger in his expression. No fury. Just love. He holds my face in his hands and smiles. "I missed you today." He gives me a kiss then grabs my ass. "Next time, please message me. I was worried."

I didn't realize I was holding my breath until I start feeling a little dizzy.

"Get changed, we're going to go for a walk on the beach before sunset."

The warm sand looks inviting. I take off my shoes and place them on a rock. Roger takes pictures as I hold up the bottoms of my pants and venture in. The incoming tide creates crashing waves around me.

"The water's a lot cooler than I expected." I turn to give him a good photo opportunity and look down to see my shoe float past me, heading out to sea.

"What the? FORD!"

"Sorry! I wasn't watching."

The tide grows stronger, bringing the waves high on shore. Roger runs to keep from getting wet. As the water retreats around me, I see my other shoe following suit.

I'm not entirely sure how it happened, but I'm suddenly thigh deep in water. I'm so engaged in trying to rescue my favorite Converse sneakers that I don't see the powerful wave coming straight for me until it's too late. It must be at least six feet high. It was a huge mistake trying to get out of the way and getting caught off-balance. "Oh, SHIT!" It hits me with such force; it knocks me off my feet and sends me to the ocean floor. When I manage to get my head back above the water level, I'm pretty sure I hear Ford laughing from the shore. At least I managed to rescue my shoes.

The pavement is burning hot from the California sun. I don't get too far off the grass before I realize I can't do this walk in bare feet. My heavy, ocean-soaked sneakers make a horrible squishing sound as I drag my feet. As we reach the front of the hotel, the bellhop asks us if we enjoyed our walk. I stop in front of him, completely soaked from head to toe and dripping. "Not really," I say unimpressed.

"Oh, I'm sorry. Let me get you a towel."

He rushes into the foyer ahead of me and grabs a pool towel from the stack at the front desk. I give Roger an annoyed look when he picks a piece of seaweed out of my hair and snickers.

I wipe the water off my face. My sneakers continue to make a sloshing sound as I trudge through the foyer. Still amused, Roger makes a comment about the puddles I'm leaving behind. I'll fix him.

"Maybe I should just strip out of these wet clothes right here?"

"Don't be silly, there are people everywhere."

I shrug. "I don't care. I'll just drop the wet ones here and wrap myself in this pool towel," I start walking toward the hotel bar, "and have a few drinks with the boys."

"Oh, no you don't." Roger reaches out and takes hold of my hand. "Do you see this hand?" He gently steers me toward the elevator. "You're going to follow wherever it leads you. And right now, it's going to lead you straight to the room."

"And what are we going to do up there?"

"I'm thinking a Pacific Coast pussy licking party."

"Uh..." Embarrassed, I glance around me to see if anyone is in earshot. "Okay."

I walk to the room like a rocket on steroids. Roger watches as I strip out of my damp clothes. "After I give that pussy a thorough licking, I'm gonna give you the big wiener."

I cringe. "Wiener? How old are you?"

He shrugs. "Two and a half."

"Thought so, I don't know too many grown men who refer to their cock as a wiener." Something catches my eye as I walk past the bedside table. "What did you do today while I was at work?"

"Not much, stayed in the room and read."

I pick up the Louis L'Amour book and look over at him astonished. "You're reading this?"

A line appears between his brows. "Yeah, why?"

"Nothing, I just." I'm not entirely sure this is a good time to bring up my father. "I just don't recall you mentioning that you enjoyed reading."

"I do." He disappears into the other room. "I marked the dirty pages, so you can read them."

I shake my head and laugh. Of course, he did.

He sticks his head around the corner. "We're definitely going to try chapter ten."

With the book in hand, I walk into the other room, flipping back to chapter ten. My face turns a scarlet red. "Oh, my."

A ghost of a smile forms on his lips. "Let's get started."

I squeal when he picks me up and folds me over his shoulder. Like a caveman, he carries me across the room and drops me on the bed. Starting at my knee, he licks and nibbles and growls his way up my thigh leaving behind a trail of pink chaffed skin from his three days' growth of stubble. I wonder if he would consider growing it into a full beard. I should ask him one day when his mouth isn't full.

Without notice, he rolls me onto my stomach and gives my ass a hard slap. The stinging sensation makes me cry out. He lays on top of me, pinning me beneath his hard, muscular body, his erection probing places it has no business exploring.

"No no no!" I say panicked. "Pick a different chapter! PICK A DIFFERENT CHAPTER!"

Chapter Eighteen

Finally, I can sleep through the night without waking up in a cold sweat from nightmares. It's a good thing the new meds are working and I'm well rested. The next few days are a whirlwind of adventure as Roger packs our evenings with whale watching tours and sightseeing drives. I've been to California a dozen times, but I've never *seen* it, until now. He has a knack for finding beautiful scenery and breathtaking landscapes.

On his last day with me in California, I can't wait to get back to the hotel to see him. There are no planned road trips or tourist destinations today. It's a warm sunny day and there's a lounge chair by the pool that has my name on it. Roger waits for me in the room, while I change into my bathing suit, acting a lot stranger than usual.

"Go on down to the pool and get a good spot. I'll meet you down there in a few minutes."

"I'll just wait for you."

"Just do what you're told for a change, would ya?"

"Okay, but why?"

"Stop asking questions. It's a surprise."

My face contorts. "I hate surprises. Remember?"

"Oh no. This one you're going to love."

Reluctantly I make my way to the pool alone. Luckily, there are two vacant lounge chairs on the sunny side of the patio. I discreetly glance at all the young, beautiful, bikini-clad women around me. Perhaps leaving Roger here all day unaccompanied is a bad idea.

A few minutes turns into forty and I'm getting concerned. I'm just about to text him when the hotel doors open and he walks, somewhat uncomfortably, into the pool area.

Concern washes over me as I watch him take very careful steps, keeping his feet shoulder-width apart. He looks a little pale.

I get to my feet, to go to his aid. "Did you hurt yourself?"

"Not exactly," he says, refusing my help.

"You look like you're in a lot of pain."

He winces as he sits beside me. "My balls are on fire."

"Umm...errrr...huh?"

"I was thinking about your friend, Goggles. I thought...I like blow jobs, so maybe I better look after the manscaping."

My eyebrows rise. I'm almost afraid to ask. "What did you do?"

"I Naired my nuts."

I gasp out loud and then burst into laughter. Several people look in our direction. I hold my hand over my mouth, trying to compose myself.

Roger gives me a dirty look. "You think it's funny, do ya?"

"Yes!" I snort, "Yes, I do. Like you found the wave attack funny." I wipe a small tear from my eyes. "I'm sorry."

"It's not funny at all, they're sweating and it stings." He grimaces as he indiscreetly adjusts his package. I can't help it. I burst into another fit of laughter.

"Glad I'm here for your entertainment pleasure," he grumbles.

The clink of glass on the table beside me makes me turn and look.

"There you go. I hear you're a mojito girl."

Still trying to get a grip, I snort and look over at Roger for an explanation.

"This is Steve. We've been hanging out today."

"Nice to meet you, Steve."

"Enjoy. I'll be right back with some appetizers."

I watch as he disappears inside. "Look at you," I tease Roger. "Making new friends while I'm slaving away at work." I take a large sip of the mojito and my eyes water. "Holy crap!"

"A little strong?"

"Oh, yes...but it's the best mojito I've ever had."

I pass him the glass so he can taste. He whistles and shakes his head. "See? I knew Steve was a good guy. He's trying to get me laid."

"Like you weren't getting laid anyway," I scoff.

"I'm not tipping him though. He steered me wrong with the whole Nair thing."

I bite my tongue. "Let's just hope that I don't pass out before I get to check everything out."

When Steve returns with the appetizers, I hand him my empty glass. "Another?" he asks.

"Yes, please. And one for Mr. Ford too, we need to extinguish a fire," I snicker.

Steve glances over at Roger.

"Just keep them coming," he confirms, as he hands me the plate of appetizers. "You better get something in your stomach besides lime and mint leaves."

I pick and nibble at the goodies on the plate. "I'm not looking forward to tomorrow."

"Neither am I. Let's not think about it and have a good time tonight."

The afternoon sun is blistering hot and I'm a thirsty girl.

I'm not sure how many times Steve returns with refreshments, but I'm starting to feel a little fuzzy. Roger is too, I think. I just watched him spend five minutes trying to pick up an olive with one of those little plastic swords. I'm not entirely sure where he got it from, but I'm sure it's compliments of his good buddy, Steve. The last mouthful pushes me into that alcohol-induced mushy mood. "When did you know?"

Roger looks at me confused. "Know what?"

"That I was *the one?*"

He leans back in his lounge chair and reminisces. "I knew the very first moment that I looked into your eyes. There's just something about them."

My heart skips a beat. Sitting upright, he takes my hand and pulls it to his lips, kissing each knuckle. "I love you."

I like hearing those three words, but I'm distracted by the fact that I can't feel my nose. Booze clouds my thoughts and kick-starts my hormones. "You do?" I touch the end of my nose and giggle.

"Yes, I do," he insists.

"How do you know it's love?"

"Because." He places his hand heavily on his heart. "Because I feel it...RIGHT...HERE."

Roger sits on the edge of the lounge chair, feeling a little emotional. He runs his fingers through my tangled hair and tucks it behind my ear. "I'm going to marry you, one day."

Whoa! I wasn't expecting that. Now I'm going to cry. Stupid mojitos!

"I can't right now," he continues. "But when I can, you'll be the fourth person to know."

Oh, dear Lord, he's going to ask my kids' permission. I struggle, not knowing what to say and terrified, knowing if he asked me at this moment I would say *yes*.

"We should go get dressed for dinner," he suggests.

"That's a great idea." It takes me three tries to get to my feet, but there's nothing graceful about it. Steve's mojitos packed one hell of a punch.

A good dinner helps to sober me up some, but Roger enjoys a few more beers. The hallway to our room seems to have tripled in length while we were at the restaurant. I don't think we're ever going to get there. I trip over the scattered bathing suits and towels just inside the door. I didn't have the foresight to hang them up or leave a light on.

If Roger had planned on this being a romantic evening, it's going to be an epic fail. He tips over twice while trying to take his socks off at the end of the bed. He's gotten very quiet since we left the restaurant. Withdrawn. I thought at first it might have been the shock of seeing the bill, but I don't think that's it at all. Sadness clouds his features as he yanks off his pants and sits at the end of the bed.

I change into my nightgown and return to the room to find him staring at the floor.

"Roger?"

He slowly raises his head to look at me. "Why are you with me?" he asks, fighting back the tears.

My heart squeezes tightly in my chest because I know exactly how he's been made to feel. I've felt the same way for many years. I move to where he sits and position myself between his knees. "Because you're a good man." A tear rolls down his cheek and I wipe it away gently. "Because you're smart and you're funny."

He tries to look away, but I'm not having it. I force him to lift his chin and lock his eyes with mine. "And you deserve to be loved."

His chest expands with air as his arms band firmly around me. He lowers his cheek to my breast and for a brief moment, he lays his armor down and allows himself to shed a tear. When he seems to have settled, I gently pry myself away.

"Get into bed," I instruct. "I'll turn off the lights." When I return, Roger is under the covers and passed out cold. Slipping in beside him, I lay awake, watching him sleep. After a few minutes, I reach out to touch his skin; I think I do it just to prove that he's real. No matter how real he seems, I feel like I'm always waiting for someone to pull the chair out from under me.

I turn to face the other way and Roger follows, anchoring himself behind me. I look at him over my shoulder when he mumbles and makes a few odd sounds. Reaching around me, he searches for my boobs, and when he has them firmly in hand he sighs and then snores.

It suddenly dawns on me. If I had met Roger Ford earlier in my life journey I would have likely overlooked him as a partner. He's nothing like the men that I would usually surround myself with; those whose social circles revolve around success and careers. I certainly wasn't at the top of their list of priorities. For a few of them, I don't think I was even in the top ten. Something my dad continually warned me about.

"You're right," I whisper. "You and my dad would have been really good friends."

Roger is an easy going, down to earth kind of guy, who's more concerned with *doing* the right thing than saying the right thing. I'll admit it, I'm a girl who appreciates formality, so I had to get used to the way he openly speaks his mind. I know if my dad was here, he'd encourage me to lighten up.

There's not a thing I'd change about Roger. I love the impact he's had on my life. I love the spontaneous road trips, the random romantic moments, and I love the laughter. I could be doing absolutely nothing with Roger Ford and still have the time of my life. I love him. My dad would be so happy to see me enjoying life for a change.

I tug the blankets out from under him and squirm down the bed. It's time for me to give my inner snob a cookie and tell her to sit the fuck down and chill.

His eyes open wide when I take him in hand. Lifting the edge of the blanket, he peers in at me as I position myself between his legs. "What are you doing?"

I lick from base to tip then smile at him. "Playing with your wiener."

Chapter Nineteen

"Are you going to be okay by yourself on the flight home?" I ask concerned, on the way to the airport.

"I have to be, don't I?"

"Yes, but I'm still worried."

He lifts my hand and kisses it, holding it to his lips. "I'm going to miss you. I don't like the idea of being apart from you for so long."

"I'm afraid that it's going to happen a few times a year. But you know what we could do? You could download Skype on the tablet, and we can talk to each other every night on video."

"I don't know, you know me and technology."

"You are *not* a stupid man. You'll figure it out. Or get one of the boys to help you."

My phone rings. "Be nice," Roger says, as he reaches over and puts it on hands-free.

I shoot him daggers with my eyes before I speak. "Hi, Mom, how are you?"

"Hi, Victoria. I'm fine, dear. How have you been?"

"I'm okay. How's Bill?"

"They started him on a new medication for his blood pressure last week, and he's got arthritis in his joints something awful. I ran into Mrs. Brown last week, she said that her mother had an old remedy that's supposed to help."

"Oh, well, good luck with that."

There's a long awkward pause before she talks again. "How are the boys?"

"They're good."

"I'm sure they've changed a lot since the last time I saw them. Maybe we could stop in this weekend?"

"Oh, sorry. I'm out of town on business."

"Who's staying with the boys?"

"Nobody, they're adults now."

"Is it safe for you to be travelling alone?"

I roll my eyes. "I'm not alone, Mom. Roger is with me."

"Who?"

Rogers's forehead puckers. "You haven't told your mom about me?"

"Shhh." I give him a warning look and lower the phone from my ear. "I haven't talked to her. Watch the road!" I point at the traffic in front of us. "Roger Ford, Mom. He's my boyfriend."

"You shouldn't put your job before the well-being of your children."

"I don't." I feel myself start to get angry, and Roger places his hand on mine, trying to relax my clenched fist.

"I better go now, I'll message you when I get back."

"We'd like to come and visit."

"Soon."

"I love you, Victoria."

"Yeah, okay, bye." I disconnect the phone as quickly as I can. Roger gives me a disapproving look. "Don't judge me."

"Okay, okay. But are you ever going to forgive her?"

"I'm trying."

"That's trying?"

"Listen, you don't know how hard it is. There's so much I'd like to get off my chest, but if I go down that road I'm going to say things that I can't take back, and it's going to crush her. Then I'll have no relationship with her at all. I don't want that. I have friends who've lost their mothers and they'd give anything to have them back, even with the bad times. So for now, it's better that I keep some space between us until I get over it, or learn to keep my big mouth shut."

Roger nods, acknowledging my thoughts. "Fair enough."

♥

For two days after Roger leaves, I throw myself into this project, working around the clock. My stomach protests loudly. I intended on eating when I got back to the hotel room, but I'm so wrapped up in what I'm working on, that I logged back in and got back to it. I look down at my phone to see what time it is and panic.

It's almost eight and Roger said that he wanted to try to Skype tonight. I'll take my laptop and head down to the bar and order something to eat. We can chat from there.

His incoming call starts to ring through and I accept with video. I haven't seen him in a few days and I'm a little anxious as it connects.

"Why aren't you wearing any clothes?" I asked shocked.

He adjusts the angle of his video. "Why are you?"

"I don't know what you've heard about Skype, but normal people wear clothes."

"Where are you?"

"I'm in the bar getting something to eat. For Pete's sake, Ford. Put some clothes on, please. There are people walking around in here."

I try to shield the screen as he gets up and crosses the room buck ass naked. My manners tell me I should look away, but I take a good long look. Damn, the man is gorgeous.

"Hurry home," he says, as he returns to the screen, tying his sleep pants at the waist. "I'm lost without you."

"It's only three more days," I assure him.

"Three very long days."

"I'm sorry. I miss you, too. It's weird not having you around."

"I know. So how is the project going?"

"It's actually going really good." I can't help but get excited as I bring him up to date on my progress.

"You sound really happy."

"I like solving problems and fixing things. It makes me feel useful. Like I'm good at something. When I succeed at my job and it helps the team worldwide...it's a sense of accomplishment that's hard to describe. I'm a happy girl when my boss is pleased."

Roger smiles. "I can see that you enjoy your job."

"I do."

"You're a very smart girl. I'm very proud of you."

I get all warm and tingly. As if he can read my mind, Roger gives me a very seductive grin. "Go back up to the room. I'm going to call you back in twenty minutes. Be naked."

♥

I'm happy when I'm busy, and this project has given me some challenges that I can really sink my teeth in. I've learned so much from one of my colleagues here in the past day that I'm really excited about the possibilities.

In the middle of the day, my phone rings, and I grow concerned.

"Hey, Carson, is everything okay?"

"No. I'm sick."

He sounds dreadful. "Oh no. What's wrong?"

"My throat hurts and I have a headache."

"Do you have a fever?"

"Is one hundred and three a fever?"

I try not to sound alarmed. "Yes, Son. That's a fever."

"I coughed so hard, I threw up."

"Where are your brothers?"

"They're at work. I think I'm dying."

"I'm sorry. Make sure you're drinking lots of fluids and try to get that fever down. Take some acetaminophen. If it isn't better in the morning, you should get into the medical clinic and see a doctor."

"I'll probably be dead by then."

I stare at my phone. Did he just hang up on me? Well, I guess that's the long-distance equivalent of slamming a door.

The guilt creeps in, causing me to think about it all afternoon. I think I've read the same paragraph ten times. I grind my teeth. My mother is right, I put my job ahead of my kids. My boy is sick and I'm on the West Coast working. I could always call her to go over and look after him until I get home. I shake my head. I can't believe I just considered it. I close my laptop and pick up my phone.

Tori: I'm coming home early.
Roger: Why?
Tori: Carson is sick.
Roger: I know. Tanner told me.
Tori: You were talking to Tanner?
Roger: Yes. I went up to help him with his carburetor.
Tori: I'm going to see if I can get on a flight tonight.
Roger: You just finished telling me you were making progress and learning lots.
Tori: I am.
Roger: So stay.
Tori: I just feel like I should be there.

Roger: Relax, Mother. We're on the job.

I open the attached picture and laugh at the image of Molly standing on the end of a shopping cart, full to the top of tissues, acetaminophen, cough syrup, and chicken soup. I'm completely blown away and feeling even more guilty now.

Tori: You don't have to do that.

Roger: Tanner was going to stay home from work, but it's my day off.

Tori: It's too much to ask of you.

Roger: Would you stop worrying. It's just a cold. We're already through the checkout and on our way to your house. Molly and I got this.

I fully trust Roger's ability to look after things, but I still worry. Isn't that what mothers do best? I have a full afternoon of meetings and conference calls, but I still find myself wondering if he's doing all the right things. Understanding my maternal needs, he sends me regular updates until I can call to check up on them.

"How is he?"

"Coughing, puking, and miserable."

I scrunch up my face. "I'm so sorry you have to deal with that."

"Anything for you."

"I just hope Molly doesn't catch it."

"She isn't even here right now. Dallas and his girlfriend took her out for a walk. I think they were going to get ice cream. Tanner and I just finished mowing the lawn and fixing the broken boards on your fence."

I pause a moment, feeling like I've just gone down the rabbit hole.

"Victoria? Are you still there?"

I give my head a shake. "Yes, sorry."

"You're busy, go back to work. Everything is fine here."

"No, it's not," I laugh. "If you've got my kids fixing shit and babysitting, there's definitely something wrong."

"They're good kids."

"You are at *my* house, right?"

"Oh, stop. You've done a great job raising these boys. I'll talk to you later."

"Okay...*take care.*" I joke

"Smartass. I love you."

"I love you, too. I'll be home in a few days."

♥

When I emerge through the double glass doors into the main concourse of the Toronto International airport, Roger is waiting with flowers. I let go of my luggage and take them out of his hands. There's a mob of people behind me in a hurry to get where they're going, and I feel the pressure to keep moving and get out of their way. Roger grabs my luggage and begins to walk toward the exit.

I try to keep up with his pace, but I'm exhausted so I lag a few steps behind. A pretty blonde in a very short skirt watches him like a hungry tigress. I can feel that territorial Amazonian warrior come alive inside me. When he finds a break in the crowd, Roger stops and waits for me to catch up. I close the space between us in a few long strides and jump into his arms, wrapping my legs around his waist. I hear the luggage hit the floor as he releases the handles and holds on to me.

I didn't realize just how much I missed him until his lips part and he welcomes me home with his tongue. When he lowers me to the ground, I slide down his body, enjoying every rippling muscle along the way. I lock eyes with the pretty blonde and smile when she looks away.

"That was one hell of a hello. Looks like the new medication is helping your hip." He zips up his jacket and pulls it down to hide his erection. "Let's get you home. I have a list of things to do this weekend and making you orgasm, often, is on the top of it."

Chapter Twenty

I'm glad to be home but I'm having trouble adjusting back to the eastern time zone. After a very long day at the Mississauga office, I drop my crap at the top of the steps and trip over a pair of sneakers that I don't recognize. I can hear Carson's voice screaming loudly at the television in the family room.

"You've hooked up the PlayStation down here?" I grumble, rounding the corner.

"It was my idea; I hope you don't mind."

"Roger!"

"Hi!"

His wide smile excites me. "What are you doing here?"

"I finished early, and Mo is at dance with my mother. I thought I'd come up and surprise you. The boys and I made dinner."

I raise my eyebrows. "You did what?"

He laughs at my expression. "As soon as I'm finished kicking Carson's butt at FIFA, we can eat."

Carson rolls his eyes. "You wish."

For a moment, I feel like I should open the door and check the house number to make sure I'm in the right place. "Ummmmmmmm. I'll set the table."

"Good girl."

"Let's go," Carson demands.

As I pass by, Roger extends his lips for a kiss, not wanting to interrupt his game.

Moving back and forth from the kitchen, I can hear the chatter between them. A change in conversation stalls my entry. I want to see how it plays out.

"So what's going on with your marketing teacher?"

"She's a bitch," Carson announces.

This topic makes my blood boil, so it's better if I just stay out of the room altogether.

"Maybe so, Bud. That's the frustrating thing about not being a kid anymore. You don't have to like her, but you have to treat her with respect."

"She doesn't treat me with respect."

"Ohhhh, nice goal," Roger concedes, before getting back on topic. "I'm sorry she treats you that way."

"She thinks I'm lazy and stupid."

"She told your mom that you're very disruptive in the class."

"Yeah. Well, I'm smarter than she is."

There's a pause in the conversation and I begin to enter the room.

"Well," Roger adds, "Are you smarter than her?"

Carson laughs once. "A LOT smarter."

"So, why don't you prove her wrong then?"

"Why bother?"

"I dunno. I'd do it just to piss her off. But that's just me."

"And *that*...was the winning goal!" Carson grins.

Roger puts down the controller and heads toward the table. "Great game, I'm starving."

I place the last dish on the table. "It smells delicious."

Carson fills a plate and leaves the room. "Where are you going?" I call after him.

"To eat in my room."

"Why don't you eat at the..." The slamming door stops the conversation. "...table with us," I finish quietly. "Well, at least I know for sure I'm in the right house."

"Pardon?" Roger piles mashed potatoes onto his plate and digs in.

"Meh, never mind. This looks delicious. Thank you so much."

"I hope you don't mind me asking him to bring the game down. I just thought he might need a little time out of his room."

"I'm shocked that he did it."

"He was telling me how good he was at that game when I picked him up."

Confusion flashes across my face.

"I picked him up from basketball practice. I sent you a message. I figured since you were working late, you wouldn't be able to."

Feeling completely inadequate, I put my hands over my face. "I forgot."

"I'm sorry." Roger stares at his phone. "Looks like I forgot to hit send again."

I shake my head. "What kind of mother forgets to pick up her kids?"

"Hey, stop it." He gathers up the dishes and drops them in the sink.

"A really bad mother, that's who," I say becoming more upset.

"You're not a bad mother, you've just got a lot on your plate."

Returning to the room, he drags my luggage over to the couch. I watch as he unzips it and begins to gather up my clothes.

"What are you doing?"

"I'm going to throw them in the washing machine." He pauses and looks up at me. "You do have one, don't you?"

"Yes, but why are you doing my laundry?"

He shrugs. "You've been home for a few days. Don't you want it done and out of the way?"

Now there's a concept. I have to admit I'm pretty good at procrastinating when it comes to domestic chores, including the laundry. That's why my luggage is still sitting in the middle of the room.

"At the bottom of the basement stairs," I direct.

When he's done, he finds me sitting on the couch waiting. I coax him to join me. This weekend has left me feeling like an enamored schoolgirl. I straddle him and run my fingers through his hair, staring into his eyes. He holds my hips, occasionally gliding his hands up my sides and stopping at the swell of my breasts. Lowering my lips to his, I brush a gentle kiss there, and then another. Digging his fingers into my flesh, he anchors me to him and when he parts his lips and deepens the kiss, I feel him swell and grow beneath me.

Needing air, he turns away.

"Where are the boys?" I ask.

"Out for the night, except for Carson."

"What's wrong?" I ask, short of breath.

"I don't want them to walk in and find me assaulting their mother again." He reaches for his ringing phone.

"Hey, Mo. What's up?"

I miss those few uninterrupted days we spent away. I slide off his lap and sit beside him. Listening to his conversation is a huge invasion of his privacy, but I can hear everything.

"If Nana said no, then the answer is no," he says firmly.

I should get up and leave the room, but since I can tell that she's crying, I can't seem to bring myself to do it.

"Molly, stop crying, please. I can't understand you."

He gives me a concerned look.

I pretend to busy myself on my phone to disguise my blatant eavesdropping.

"Well, I can't do anything about it right now. You'll have to wait until I get home."

"*You're never home.*" I hear her sob.

"When I am home you don't even talk to me."

"I hate her!"

"That's not fair. This isn't Victoria's fault."

"You never bought Mommy flowers!"

Roger throws his head back and clenches his jaw tightly. His face turns red. "Molly, your mother didn't tell me she was unhappy. She just left without giving me a chance to fix it." He gets to his feet and paces.

"Roger," I try to interrupt discreetly, but he ignores me.

He raises his voice. "Stop with the drama, Mo! I mean it. I'm not coming home tonight!"

"Roger," I persist until he pauses and looks at me. "You need to go home and look after your family." I give him a small shrug and a sympathetic smile.

His blue eyes stare at me, trying to work something out. Still holding his phone to his ear, he runs his fingers through his hair and sighs.

"Molly, pack up your things. I'm coming to pick you up and take you home."

He stuffs his phone into his pocket and stands silently, staring at me. I get to my feet and wrap my arms around him.

"I'm sorry," he says aggravated. "I wanted to stay with you tonight."

"It's okay," I assure him. "I've had you all weekend and almost every day for the past week. She misses you."

"Still."

"Stop. I know all about being a Daddy's girl." I let out a small laugh and look over at my father's picture. "It's pretty much the only thing I know how to do *well*. I still feel lost without him sometimes."

I can tell by looking into his eyes that he's pleased with the small amount of my past that I've shared. I'm getting better at it. "Call me later, if you can."

He nods, still looking agitated as he heads to the door.

"Roger. Promise me you'll listen."

He narrows his eyes. "What?"

"Don't argue, don't get angry or get defensive. Just listen to what she's saying. Seems to me that we don't really *listen* to what our kids are actually saying."

He scratches his head and lets out a heavy sigh. "Okay." He leans in and kisses me. "I'll call you later."

I close the door behind him and watch through the window as he gets into his car. So much has gone on the past few weeks that my head is spinning. I need for things to be okay between Roger and his daughter. As much as I need my kids to be okay with Roger. I'm still not entirely sure we're free and clear on that count.

I pick up my e-reader and open the newest steamy novel that Jen made me download. I might as well try to relax and read about somebody else getting laid.

♥

The following day, Roger arrives at my work with lunch and a Tim Hortons Steeped Tea.

"Hi. I didn't hear from you last night. Is everything okay?"

"I did what you told me. I kept my mouth shut and just listened."

"That's good. And what did you hear?"

"That I'm not home anymore."

I nod. "You're not."

He sighs. "I know. I guess, in a way, I was enjoying being away from that house."

I can understand that. I, myself, couldn't stand to live in the home that was a constant reminder of my failed marriage. "Have you ever thought of selling the house? Getting a fresh start somewhere else?"

He scratches his eyebrow. "A few times but I didn't want to uproot her on top of everything else." He takes on a tortured expression. "But it's not just the house, Tori." He takes a deep breath. "I think I really needed some time away from my daughter."

I stop him. "Don't."

"Don't what?"

"Don't feel guilty about needing a break." I point to myself. "Single mom with three kids, remember?"

"I feel like I let her down."

Sensing his frustration, I wrap my arms around him. "Everybody needs a break from their children now and then. It doesn't mean that you don't love her. And it sure as hell doesn't mean you've failed her."

He shakes his head. "I don't know how you did it."

"I had no choice. For ten years I focused only on them. My dad said that I...*we* deserve to have other people in our life. It took me a long time to listen, but you know what? He was right. I know it's hard not to feel guilty about it. I still suffer from *single parent guilt disorder*." I give him a small smile. "We'll figure it out."

♥

Jen slides a glass across the bar table and leaves it in front of me.

"So when did you see him last?"

"He messages me every day, but I haven't seen him since Tuesday."

"Wow, a whole week. That must be tough since you were seeing him almost every day."

"I'm trying to convince myself that seeing him every day was an unhealthy, codependent thing anyway. But, yeah."

"Why is this again?" Jen finishes her vodka and cranberry and waits patiently for me to answer.

"Molly misses the things they used to do together."

"I see."

"So he promised her that he'll spend more time with her."

"So, is he going to try and juggle the two of you separately for the rest of his life?"

"What do you mean?"

Her brows draw together. "Seems to me the way it's working right now is he either spends time with you, or he spends time with her."

"It wasn't meant to be the long-term solution, but he felt it was something he needed to do right now. I guess I'll talk to him tomorrow after dinner."

My insecurities lurk close to the surface, waiting for the opportunity to come out of hibernation. Jen recognizes the angst on my face. "I'm sorry, please don't stress over it. I'm sure it'll work itself out."

I nod, but I'm not very convincing.

"Roger isn't like the other guys, Tori. He really seems to adore you."

"I'm wondering now, if he loves *me* or if he just likes the idea of being in love. Everything just happened so fast."

Being in a relationship again is absolutely terrifying. I'm not entirely sure I remember how to be in one, but this doesn't feel right. There have been men in my life over the years, and I tried to convince myself that I was okay with the occasional booty calls, for the lack of a better term. At the time, I reasoned that an uncommitted relationship was safer for me. No strings, no disappointments, and no heartache. There was also no companionship, no respect, and no intimacy. Just sex. Funny that I chose those relationships, thinking they would protect me from being hurt again, but in a way, they made the hurt so much worse by strengthening my deep-seated belief that I'm not worthy of love.

Roger made me believe that I am. I have no idea how this is going to play out, but I'm worried.

Chapter Twenty-One

I can't wait to see Roger. The traffic gods are smiling on me today, so I manage to get there in record time. I won't tell him how fast I drove, but I'm pretty proud of myself. I find it odd that he doesn't come out to meet me. I push open the door and peek in. "Hello?"

Roger comes up the basement stairs with a basket full of clean laundry. "Hi. Sorry, baby. I didn't think you'd be here for another fifteen minutes or so." Recognition dawns on his face. "You promised me you'd slow the fuck down."

I try to look innocent, but it doesn't work. He shakes his head. "I give up. I'll just take this basket upstairs and be right back."

I nod. "Is there anything I can do to help with dinner?"

"No. It's been a fuck of a day. I thought we could order something in."

I look around the living room and I can't put my finger on it, but something's different. It isn't until I sit down on the couch and turn on the TV that I realize that several family portraits have reappeared in the room.

"Where's Molly?" I ask when he returns.

"I sent her to my sister's."

"Because I'm here?" I consider his silence an admission of guilt. "You said we need to talk things through, right?"

He narrows his eyes. "Yes."

"Okay, so here it goes...I feel like we're kind of going backwards here."

"What do you mean?"

"You said you were ready to move on."

"I am."

I so desperately want to believe him, but there's something in his expression that tells me that's not true.

"It's been a rough couple of days, and I didn't want to bother you with my shit."

I recognize this is a reversal of roles. "Isn't that what people in relationships do?" I ask. "Help each other with their shit."

Truly not himself today, he shrugs.

"So tell me what's going on," I urge.

"I got a letter from my wife's lawyer yesterday."

"You mean your ex-wife?"

"Not yet."

My eyes widen. "Excuse me?"

His expression goes blank. "We aren't legally divorced."

"Well, fuck." I search my memory, but I can't actually recall him ever saying he was, so maybe I just assumed so. I glance around the room at the pictures.

He answers my unasked question. "Molly asked me to put them back up. Do they make you feel uncomfortable?"

"No," I lie, and it shows on my face. "A little."

"I'm sorry. This must be hard for you."

"Ya think?" Anxiety and mistrust begin to build within me and it's time we get to the bottom of things. "Why did your wife leave?"

His jaw tightens. "She left me for another man."

I can't bring myself to ask why. There's always a reason someone falls out of love and each one is as valid as the next. Sometimes you can love someone with all your heart, and it isn't enough to make a relationship work. I know that for a fact.

"I wasn't good enough," he continues, growing angrier. "The day she told me she was in love with someone else, she ruined my life."

I reach out to comfort him, but he takes a few steps away from me, massaging the throbbing vein in his neck.

"You had no clue?"

"No! None. I thought we were happy. I was happy!"

"No, sweetheart. If you had no clue that she was falling in love with another man, you didn't have a very good relationship. You were probably comfortable with your life: content with your situation, but you weren't happy. Not as a couple." I wish I could love his hurt away. "You must have been devastated when she told you."

"I didn't handle it very well at all. I completely lost my mind. I called her names and told her to get all her stuff and get out of the house."

Curiosity pushes me to ask questions I don't want the answers to. "Do you still love her?"

"No, I don't still love her." His forehead creases. "Why would you ask me that?"

"Because you're still really angry about it."

He picks up papers and hands them to me. "I love *you*. I'm angry because of this."

I read through them, trying to decipher all the legal mumbo-jumbo.

"She wants me to sell the house and give her half, as well as half of my pension, and spousal support until she retires," he summarizes.

"What about Molly? There's nothing in here about custody or child support."

Roger takes the paper out of my hand and folds it in half. "The day she left, she stood at the front door and told me that I was a worthless piece of shit and that Molly reminded her so much of me, that she couldn't stand to look at her. I slammed the door in her face, and when I turned around, Molly was standing on the stairs behind me."

I get a sick feeling in the pit of my stomach. "Oh my God, that poor girl."

"So I hope you'll understand that she needs me."

"Of course." What else can I say?

"I need to spend more time with her. I'm so sorry."

"That's how it should be."

"Things don't have to change between you and me."

Then why does it feel like I'm being thrown away again? I squash those 'F' word responses down deep inside and nod. "Of course not."

"I just need you to know what I'm dealing with right now."

We eat dinner in front of the TV and try to conduct our evening with some normalcy. It isn't easy since that bomb has left me feeling somewhat shell-shocked. Roger pulls me against his chest and strokes my hair. There's an uncomfortable tension between us. For the first time ever, I think we put on a movie and *actually* watch the movie. After turning off the lights and locking all the doors, Roger gets into bed, gives me a quick peck on the lips, and rolls to face the opposite direction. I lay there for hours, wide-awake, my brain racing in a million different directions.

♥

Roger tries hard to divide up his time over the next few weeks, but it's taking a toll on both of us. It's hard to watch all the Facebook updates of their times together while I sit home alone. I feel selfish, petty, and ashamed. I throw myself back into my work to keep me distracted. Roger tries to call me as often as he can, but it's not the same.

It doesn't take long before I realize that he and Molly are hiking with friends, shopping with his parents, and having dinner with the neighbors. In other words, this isn't special Daddy/Daughter time. This is time spent with his daughter that includes other people, just not *me*.

I feel it all starting to slip away. My time with him dwindles down to a few lunches during the week and an hour or two while she's at dance. There's an aching in my chest that I haven't felt for some time. That old protective wall starts to build up, preparing itself for heartbreak.

I know that he and Molly have plans for tonight, but I need to see him. I pull in front of the house at the same time as his sister.

"Oh, oh. I think I need to go home and change," she jokes as she gets out of the car.

"Why?"

"Look at you, you're all dressed up."

"I'm just coming from work."

"I thought you were kind of overdressed for bowling," she laughs.

"Oh. I'm not going bowling."

"Not your thing?"

I purse my lips. "No, I wasn't invited."

"Of course you're invited. We're all going. Why wouldn't you be invited?"

I feel the tears pool in my eyes. "I guess you need to ask your brother."

Her brow creases. "Victoria? Is everything okay?"

I frown, "I'm sorry. I should get home."

Roger joins Jackie at the end of the driveway and watches as I drive away.

Hurt would best describe the **F**-word that I'm experiencing right now, and I hate him for it.

♥

The following day, Roger calls but I ignore it. I send him a text to tell him that I'm busy with meetings and that I'll talk to him later. Then I turn off my phone, so I don't have to deal with him. I need some time. I know that he's at work today, so I won't have to worry about him showing up.

I'm thankful for call display when he starts to call my office phone. The next three times he calls, I let it go to voicemail and try to get some work done. He certainly is persistent; I'll give him that. It's the most effort he's given me in days.

I watch the clock, waiting for my next call to begin. The phone rings and I answer the unknown number, assuming it's the conference leader ready to begin. I'm surprised by his sneakiness.

"You're screening your calls so you don't have to talk to me?"

"Of course not, Roger, I've just been busy today."

"I thought we agreed that we'd talk things out."

"There isn't anything to talk out. It's all good."

"You must think I'm pretty stupid to believe that."

"Not at all. I just have a lot to do today."

"Can I see you tonight?"

"No, I'm sorry. It's Wednesday night, I'm going out with Jen."

"Victoria, I'm sorry about last night."

Anxiety runs through me; I don't want to talk about it right now. My dad once told me that relationships are a journey full of compromise. If you can't meet in the middle, then you should take a different road altogether. Right now, I'm thinking I should just let things start to fade out. There's less collateral damage that way. It seems impossible that we could ever coexist, and I would never make him choose.

"It's okay, I understand. You need to put your daughter first. I have to go; my conference call is starting. Take care."

My hand shakes as I hang up the phone. This day just needs to end.

♥

Jen and Anna flank me from either side on the dance floor, worried that I've done a lot more drinking than dancing so far tonight. I'll admit that I'm enjoying the carefree numbness, and I'm beginning to remember why I kept myself so closed off for many years. It's easier when you don't have any feelings or pain.

"So what are you going to do?" Anna asks when we make our way back to the table.

"I have no idea."

"Do you love him?"

I must, because even the question makes my heart ache. "I do, but does it matter?"

"I think you need to sit his ass down and talk it out," Anna says.

"I'm still rooting for the nice guy," Jen adds.

"But everything's changed."

"Nothing has changed," Jen argues. "It's a bump in the road. Tell him how you feel and give him a chance to fix it."

I laugh once. "Fix what? His daughter? That little girl has been through so much. I'm not going to be the reason she needs lifelong therapy."

"No, Tori. Her mother is going to be the reason for that. Don't give up; she'll come around eventually. I guarantee it. You and Roger are meant to be together. You told me he was the love of your life."

"He is. But what do I do in the meantime? Sit around and wait for him to squeeze me in?"

"I don't know, but you better figure it out fast," Jen says glancing over my shoulder. "He's here."

I can feel his presence behind me, so I get to my feet and face him. Stress has clouded his rugged good looks. I'd be surprised if he's had any sleep at all in the past week. He looks haggard. His normally bright blue eyes look heavy and dull grey. "We need to talk," he demands in a raspy voice.

I lift my drink to my mouth and chug it down, then slam the empty glass on the table. "Sure. Let's talk."

Jen partially covers her face with her hand and gives me a disapproving look.

He surveys the loud, busy room. "Can we go outside where it's quiet?"

"Yes, we can do that."

I catch him glance over at Jen, and she gives him a warning look. My first step is a little wobbly, and he grabs my elbow for support.

"How much have you had to drink?"

"Only two."

Anna holds up two fingers on one hand, and five on the other.

"I'm perfectly fine." I pull my elbow out of his grip. "I don't need your help."

He holds his hands up in defeat. "Okay, I'm sorry."

He follows closely as I make my way out to the parking lot. The cool evening air is sobering. I lean against the trunk of his car and cross my arms.

He stares at me, unsure of where to start. "I don't like what's going on right now."

"Pffft, do you think I do?" I scoff.

"Talk to me."

"I don't know where I fit in anymore."

"The same place you always did."

I shake my head. "No. I don't. I get that you need to spend time with your daughter. She needs you. But is there any reason why I can't be part of that, too? Couldn't we be doing stuff together, so she and I can get to know each other better?"

From the expression on his face, I'm about to see the Irish temper he warned me about. "I don't know!" he yells. "I don't have any clue what the fuck I'm doing! I just want everyone to be happy." He paces a few steps, clenching his fists at his sides. "If you wanted to join us, why didn't you say something? You've got a voice!" he growls.

"It didn't feel like you wanted me around."

"Of course I want you around. Do you think that I've just been stringing you along for good times?"

I stare past him, avoiding his gaze.

"DO YOU?" he shouts.

I grind my teeth and meet with his icy stare. "No."

He rakes his hands through his hair and holds his head. "I can't fucking win here! What am I supposed to do?"

"Nothing," I say defeated. "You do nothing."

"For fuck's sake, Tori," he yells. "What do you want?"

I don't know how to answer that. The numbness masks the broken heart and it's sending me mixed signals. I'm torn between the love of my life and a small fragile girl who needs her father. Just as I needed mine.

"Well?" Answer me."

"I just want a normal life. No drama. No anxiety." I take a stuttered breath, trying to keep my emotional responses at bay. "I don't want to worry about who my kids are hanging out with, or how I'm going to pay for their post-secondary educations. For once, I'd like to have a conversation with one of them without having a door slammed in my face."

Roger takes a rigid stance in front of me, his jaws clenched tightly while waiting out my rant.

My voice sticks in the back of my throat, making the words come out no louder than a whisper. "I want my dad back." I dab my nose with a tissue from my pocket. "And I want to feel appreciated and loved."

His crestfallen expression tears a hole in my heart. "Are you telling me that you don't feel wanted?"

I lock my eyes to his and swallow down the pain. I refuse to cry.

"No, I don't."

He bangs his fist down hard on the trunk beside me. "So what are you saying? Do you want to break up?"

The desire to fight leaves me and he's just given me an out. "Yes. I think it's best."

Looking defeated, he scratches his beard and nods. There is no angry outburst or argument. There is no objection or plea. He just simply opens the car door and leaves. I move out of the way, watching as the ZL1 backs out and rumbles past me. Panic hits me hard in the chest as I'm illuminated by the glow of the bright red brake lights when he reaches the road. What am I doing? I hold my head in disbelief and pace a few steps. I can feel his eyes burning into me and I look up to find him staring at me in the rearview mirror. His pained expression cuts me deep like a sharp blade. I've made a mistake, and I can't let him go. I call out, trying to stop him, but my voice is masked by the roaring V8 engine and the squeal of tires. When the smoke settles, he's gone, and the tears find their way.

Chapter Twenty-Two

Fresh air and lots of coffee sober me up before Jen lets me get behind the wheel, but I still drive home in a fog. Not the kind of fog caused by warm and cool weather systems colliding. The kind of fog that consumes your thoughts and feelings and numbs them to a level where you're barely aware that they exist. I make the drive from the bar in Norval, all the way to Dufferin County, and I have no idea how I got here. The heavy rain clouds hide the stars, and the dark sky mirrors my mood. I hurry into the house to avoid getting wet from the downpour that starts the moment I open the car door.

I leave my storm-soaked clothes in a pile on the floor, crawl in under the covers and lay listening to the storm. Lightning brightens the sky, challenging the clouds for dominance of the stars. Thunder rolls angrily through the night, refusing to surrender. The turbulent emotions churning inside of me seem to be embodied in the intractable storm. Falling tears preface a sobbing cry that, like the storm, doesn't want to let up. Years of anger and regret flood to the surface but it doesn't erase the intense hurt and pain.

Then something strange happens, an ethereal feeling of calm washes over me, lightening the heavy weight on my chest. The storm rolls off into the distance and the light from the reappearing stars shines through the bedroom window. Maybe it's a deeply seated survival mechanism, or maybe it's my father watching over me. The silence makes me feel *at peace*, and I know that I'm going to be okay. That's what I do, it's what I always do...I survive.

♥

It's amazing how much work I can get done when I don't have any *dick*stractions. In just a few days, I plow my way through millions of lines of data validation with razor sharp focus. Something I'm hoping to continue until I look down at an incoming message.

From Roger: I NEED YOU

I delete it from my phone and get back to my project. Jen calls, just to check in and I assure her all is well. In fact, they are fantastic, but I can tell she doesn't believe me.

I return from my one o'clock meeting and try to refocus.

From Roger: I WANT YOU

I look to the heavens and take a deep breath. Why is he doing this to me?

From Roger: I CRAVE YOU

I growl and remove them from my phone. NOW he figures out how to send simple, coherent text messages? I jump when my phone rings. I try to calm my racing heart as I hesitantly look at the screen. It races even faster when the display reads Westside Secondary School. I grab it quickly before it goes to voicemail.

"This is Victoria."

"Mrs. Campbell, this is Susan Cantwell. Carson's marketing teacher."

My mind considers all the things that he could have done wrong. "Yes, how are you?"

"I'm sorry to bother you, but I wanted to talk to you about Carson's last marketing project."

"Is he late handing it in?"

"No, it was on time."

"Did he fail?"

"No. Actually, I'm phoning to tell you that your son received 110% on this assignment."

"I'm confused."

"So am I, to be quite honest. There were two parts to this assignment. Your son found an error in the logic in the textbook on sales profitability. He answered the questions appropriately and then added a note that said, 'These are the answers you're looking for, however, this would be inaccurate.' On the back page of the assignment, he defined the error in the logic and answered all the questions with the correct values."

I laugh once. "You're kidding me?"

"No, Mrs. Campbell. I'm not. The second part of the assignment was an essay style project on marketing ethics and practices. It was so well thought out and written I was certain that he plagiarized it."

Ah, here it comes. "And was it?"

"I spent three days on the internet and in the library trying to find proof of it. But I couldn't. I've taught college classes and never received a report this good."

"You believe he did the work himself?" Now I'm suspicious.

She pauses. "Yes, I do. I know that Carson and I have had some problems in class, but now I understand. Mrs. Campbell your son is very gifted. This is brilliant work. I can't help but wonder..."

"Why he's in the applied courses?" I interrupt.

"Yes."

"It's an epic parenting fail. After I left his father, and his grandfather passed away, Carson became lost: disinterested. I tried to get him into special courses, but he dug in his heels and chose to fail. Your school guidance counselors allowed him to drop all his classes without my knowledge."

"To be honest, I'm new to the school so I didn't know him before this year. I wasn't aware of his potential."

"Because he dresses like a gangster and he disrupts the class, you assumed he wasn't a kid deserving of your time."

"I'm so sorry."

"I understand. You have little time and a lot of students. Your focus needs to be on those who are interested in doing well and wanting to learn. His attitude shows the opposite."

"It's a very important lesson for me. I hope not to repeat the same mistakes in the future. Now that I have his attention, I'll do my best to keep him engaged and challenged."

I'm well aware this has everything to do with his conversation with Roger. I realize for the first time just how much Carson and I are alike. "Thank you, for your call."

My cell phone vibrates on my desk and I immediately regret glancing down at the message.

From Roger: I LOVE YOU

Emotions start to bubble within me, like lava escaping from the mouth of hell. I'm bitten from every direction as I fight off the two-headed hellhound of feelings.

"I don't love you," I whisper out loud, as I delete him from my contacts and block his number. I follow suit on Facebook and every other social media account he could use to message me before I go home.

♥

I groan when I turn onto my street and see the blue Dodge parked out front. The last thing I need today is to deal with my mother. She's sitting at the kitchen table knitting. "Hello."

She looks at me over the edge of her glasses. "Hello, Victoria."

"Why are you here?"

"I wanted to see you, and if I waited for you to invite me, I'd never get the chance."

"Chance to what?"

"Talk to you."

"About?"

"Bill."

I make a cup of tea and place it down in front of her. "Is Bill okay?"

"Oh heavens, yes. He's fine. We're happy."

I don't know why but that makes my heart feel heavy. "So what did you want to talk about?"

"Victoria, I know you've carried this anger around with you for a lot of years, and I think it's time we talked."

My heart starts to flutter nervously in my chest. "Okay." I pull out a chair and join her.

"I'm so very sorry you feel that I betrayed your father."

I feel the tension knot in my shoulders. "You did."

"I loved your father."

I laugh once. "You have a strange way of showing it."

"Your father was a good man. And we did love each other. Sometimes in our lives, things happen that we can't control. Bill was my first love. My soul mate. We lost touch when he left town to attend college.

That's when I met your father. The universe has a way of making things right."

I blink my eyes a few times, trying to get my head around her statement. "Are you saying that Dad was a mistake? And that he died so you could be with Bill?"

"No. Not at all. Every moment with your father was a blessing. That doesn't mean we didn't have our troubles and our regrets."

She lifts her teacup to her mouth and takes a small sip, reflecting on something.

"When your brother became completely consumed by his addiction, it was a very difficult time for us. Your father somehow felt it was his fault. He spent all of our savings, and every penny we had put away for our retirement, trying to get the boy some help and into rehab. Nothing worked."

I listen, in awe to a side of the story I've never heard.

"Feeling like a failure, your dad dealt with it by drinking. He completely pushed me away. When Bill came back into my life, I was heartbroken and lonely, feeling like I had lost both a son and a husband."

"What about me, Mom? Did you ever think about me?"

She gives me a small comforting smile and places her hand on top of mine. "Even at a very young age, you were strong and fierce. You were the one person I never worried about, Victoria. I always knew no matter what life threw at you, you'd land on your feet."

"That doesn't mean that I didn't need you to lean on sometimes, Mom."

"I know that now."

My face turns red. "When I left my husband, I took three small children out of the house in the middle of the night, and you have never asked me why!"

She frowns and looks away a moment. "I'm sorry. I made some very selfish decisions. Even parents sometimes make mistakes. I hope it's not too late. Bill and I want to be involved in your life. We want to be around for the boys."

Now she's hit a nerve. Anger starts to pump through my veins. I'm so angry I feel like I'd like to throw something. I get to my feet and pace the kitchen floor, trying to decide what to do. "I can't. I just can't deal with this right now, Mom."

"Okay, I understand, I just thought it was time you heard it."

I bite my tongue so hard I'm surprised I don't draw blood.

"Will I get to meet Roger soon?"

"Roger and I broke up."

She gets to her feet and gathers up her knitting. "Always pushing people away, afraid to love." She shakes her head and throws her knitting bag over her shoulder. Stopping at the door, she turns and gives me a knowing smile. "You love the man. I'm still your mother so I can tell. Forgive him, Tori. For whatever it is he's done. Or hasn't done. Life is too short to hold grudges. Live your life so that it's a love story worth sharing with the world." She opens the door and steps out onto the porch. "Maybe one day, you'll be interested in hearing mine."

I don't know if I'm going to laugh or cry. I'm feeling completely overwhelmed. "Thanks for stopping by."

"Okay, I'm leaving. Just know I love you."

I close the door and lean against it, ensuring it's closed tight.

"MOM!"

"I'm right here, Tanner. You don't need to yell."

"Is Roger here? We bought a new part for my transmission and it was delivered today. He's going to help me fix it."

I'm not sure just how much more I can handle today. "No, Son. I'm afraid Roger won't be coming around anymore."

He narrows his eyes. "Why? What's going on?"

"We broke up."

He processes the information and frowns at me. "Why?"

I shrug. "It just wasn't going to work out."

"What about Molly? Roger said she has a dance recital coming up, shouldn't you be there for her?" I looked at him, stunned.

"Roger brought her up here a few times when you were away. She's kind of a cool kid when you look past the part that she's an annoying little girl."

"I'm afraid I won't be going to any recitals."

"He got too close, so you're pushing him away."

"Tanner, you have no clue what I'm going through right now. Please, don't call him anymore.

I stare at him until he opens his contacts and blocks Roger's number. He shakes his head in disapproval. "So that's it?"

I look away avoiding his censure. "Yes, that's it."

"You're just going to let him go?"

I nod. "You're the man of the house, again."

Tired of dealing with this emotional upheaval, I get ready for bed. The moment I sit on the edge of the bed my eyes begin to close. I don't even remember climbing in and shutting off the light.

Thunder roars and wakes me up. The curtains blow wildly, and I climb out of bed and try to close the window. The driving rain is puddled on the floor. I wander down the hallway, investigating a noise downstairs. I pause at the bottom, staring at the figure leaning against the kitchen counter with his ankles crossed. "Hi, Dad."

"Hi, Victoria."

"What are you doing here?"

"Watching over you."

"I can look after myself."

"Oh no you can't, my love. Your mother's right."

"About what?"

"You're a stubborn girl."

I frown and he smiles. "Stop pouting."

"What should I do, Dad?"

"Forgive them."

"It's not that easy."

"It is that easy, Tori. Just let it go. It's time to let love in."

I open my eyes and look around the room. Instinctively, I reach out for Roger, but find his place cold and empty. I'd probably allow myself to shed a few tears, but there's a frantic pounding on my bedroom door.

Chapter Twenty-Three

I open the door to find Tanner standing on the other side, looking conflicted.

"Is everything, okay?"

"Have you heard from Dallas?"

I pick up my phone and check my messages. "No. Why?"

"I don't know how to tell you this."

"What Tanner?"

"Okay, don't freak out."

"Telling me not to freak out is a sure way to make me freak out! What's going on?"

"Dallas went with Eddie to a party tonight."

"I thought he wasn't hanging out with that guy anymore?"

"Yeah, I figured he didn't tell you."

"I'll talk to him when he gets home."

His expression makes me nervous. "Tanner?"

"It's all over Facebook. There were a lot of sketchy people at that party. The police showed up," he pauses. "There were shots fired. The word all over social media is that there were fatalities."

"What time is it?"

"After midnight."

I dial his number.

"I've already tried, Mom. He's not answering."

"Where's Carson?"

"He's in his room, studying. He hasn't heard from him either."

"Thank God he isn't with him this time."

My phone rings. *Unknown Number.* I just can't deal with Roger right now so I ignore the call. I grab my keys off the table. "What's the address? I'm going over there."

"I was already there. The cops have the neighborhood locked down tight. I couldn't get close."

"You're not a frantic mother. Get your brother, you're both going with me."

I drive like a mad woman, determined to find my way through the maze of roadblocks. Frustrated, I put the car in park in the middle of the street and get out. I catch a glimpse of the coroner and my hands begin to tremble. On every corner, the authorities have corralled kids and hold them for questioning. There's no sign of Dallas or Eddie.

I stand at the barricade, feeling helpless. "Excuse me, officer. I'm looking for my son."

"You and about three hundred other parents," he says stoically. "Go back home and wait there. I'm sure he'll be home soon."

I don't like being dismissed. I take out my phone and dial his number again. A few feet away, on the hood of a police car, a phone begins to ring. My eyes open wide.

"Please," I beg. "Check to see if it's his."

One of the officers wanders over and picks it up, turning the screen so I can see it. Tanner and Carson arrive at my side. Fear washes over me and my tone escalates. "Why do you have my son's phone?"

"It was found at the scene."

"Mom." Tanner directs my attention to the front door where the coroner escorts out body bags. Three of them. Panic starts to set in, and I push the barrier out of the way and shoulder past the guards. Carson and Tanner are detained by a burly policeman before they can follow me. An officer grips me firmly by the elbow, stopping me. "Is that my son?" I scream, becoming completely unglued.

"Ma'am, you need to go home and let us do our job."

I flail and thrash, trying to break free. "Why won't you answer me? Is my son dead?"

He gives my arm a hard tug and pulls me off to the side. "Listen to me, Momma. I get you're worried, but you're scaring your other two boys."

I glance over at them and try to take a calming breath.

"His name is Dallas." I plead desperately. "He was at this party with his friend, Eddie."

The two officers exchange a grim look when I mention his name. "PLEASE! Just tell me."

"One of the victims wasn't carrying any ID. We're still investigating."

He escorts us back to the car. "Go home and wait there. In the meantime contact all his friends and see if anyone has information."

"If you don't hear from us, then consider that a good sign."

All the way home, Carson and Tanner busy themselves with their phones. If anybody knows something, they'll find out. I drive past a few of his favorite hangouts to see if he's there, but no one has seen him today. I check my phone constantly, but there's nothing except another missed call from the same unknown number. My heart feels like it's in a vice grip.

It's been almost an hour and I pace back and forth across the living room floor. I can't lose someone else I love. I won't survive it.

The door pushes open and I hold my breath. Dallas walks in, looking pale and exhausted. The boys jump to their feet.

"Thank God you're okay." I pull him into a tight hug as he breaks down. I hold him tighter and comfort him. Tears stream down my cheeks. I'm so caught up in having my boy home I didn't even notice that Roger is standing in the doorway behind him.

Dallas pulls out of my arms, only to be snatched up in an embrace by his older brother. "You scared the shit out of me, man," Tanner says, trying to hide his emotions. "I'll kick your ass if you ever pull anything like that again."

"Everybody has been looking for you," Carson adds.

"Why didn't you call?" I holler.

"I did, you didn't answer."

"Then you should have called your brothers!"

Roger interrupts. "Go easy on the boy, Mother. He's had a rough night."

I close my eyes and take a deep breath. Roger's right. Dallas' expression hardens. I know he's trying to stop himself from breaking down again. "Eddie is dead."

I nod. "I know. Go upstairs with your brothers and start letting everyone know that you're home safe. We'll talk later."

"Can you order a pizza from Johnny's?" he asks halfway up the stairs. "I'm starving."

I give him a reassuring smile. "Sure, I'm on it."

Roger still stands in the doorway, not sure if he's welcome. "I tried to call you. You blocked my number. I figured you probably made Tanner delete me, too."

I look guilty and he rolls his eyes.

I sigh heavily. "Come in." I wait for him to join me in the living room. "I thought about calling you, but I was afraid if I heard your voice, I would have lost it all together."

"That's why I decided to just bring him home."

"Thank you, for that. Did he tell you what happened?"

"His buddy was involved in some very serious drug trafficking that he claims he knew nothing about until they got there. He didn't want any part of it, so he had his phone in his hand to call Tanner and was on his way out of the house when the cops raided. He turned and watched as Eddie took a gun out of his pocket and raised it. They took him down with several shots. People panicked and scrambled. Someone bumped into him, knocking his phone out of his hand."

I listen to the story, with my hand over my mouth. This only happens on television. How is it possible that my family has just been through this? This is a small community where it's supposed to be safe to raise your babies.

Roger reaches out to touch me then stops himself. "A bunch of them jumped into a buddy's car and took off, and they kept driving until they ran out of gas out in the middle of nowhere."

"How did you..." I frown, not needing to finish my question. I already know. Roger bonded with my boys. They adored him. They needed him, and I took him away from them, too.

"He borrowed someone's phone and called me." He watches my expression, not sure how I'm going to react. "Right after he gave me their location the battery went dead."

"Thank you, for taking his call."

"Why wouldn't I?"

I'm not quite sure how to respond, so I shrug. "You didn't have to."

"Just because you don't want me around anymore doesn't mean that I won't help your kids if they need me," he says, becoming agitated. "I love your kids like they're my own. I'd do anything for them. I'd still do anything for you. Why don't you get that?"

Everything starts to weigh down on me all at once, and I feel my bottom lip start to tremble.

"I know this is the wrong time to bring it up, but fuck, when have I ever done anything at the right time?"

"I don't want to fight with you tonight," I say quietly.

He pauses. "Tori, we have to talk about it. I'm miserable without you. Don't tell me that you're happy. I know you're not. Tanner told me that he heard you cry yourself to sleep last night."

"Well, that wasn't something he should have shared."

Roger becomes more upset. "How ridiculous is it that your eighteen-year-old son has more emotional maturity than you?"

That one hurt. I look away, fighting back the tears.

"Look at me," he demands angrily. He reaches for me, but I pull away. "You're not shutting me out this time. Damn it, Victoria. I'm not perfect but I know how to love. And I know how to take care of you."

It's too painful to have this conversation, but I'm stuck beneath some invisible force that stops me from walking away.

"And I know how to look after your family if you'll just let me be part of it."

"But Molly..."

He stops me. "Molly is a little girl, who's terrified because she thinks if she loves somebody, they're going to go away." He raises his brows. "Sound familiar?"

I nod.

"I thought I was doing the right thing, trying to protect her. We had a long talk, her and I. I don't want to live my life without you. Molly understands now. To be honest, we both need you."

I hold my hand on my heart, trying to keep it together.

"And my sister...well, she can't even look at me without cursing."

I try to talk, but nothing comes out.

"Victoria, what I'm trying to say is...life is hard. Relationships are hard. We need to talk about stuff; work through things. Look after each other. Nobody else is going to." Determined to convince me, he reaches out and takes hold of my arms. "I REFUSE!!"

I watch the tears glisten in his eyes and finally find my voice. "Refuse to what?"

"Expire. I refuse to expire," he says emotionally, running his hands up and down my arms. "I know I fucked up. I'm sorry," he says regretfully.

I can't hold back the tears another minute.

"Hey." He moves closer and brushes his fingers across my cheek. "Look at me, please."

I raise my gaze to his beautiful blue eyes and let his touch remind me how it feels to be loved.

"Put the tears away," he whispers, softly. "Everything is okay now. Your boy is home and so am I."

I nod my acceptance. I've craved this moment since the minute I let him drive away. I miss him. I squeeze my eyes shut, forcing out the tears.

"Give the guy a break, would ya?" I hear Tanner say.

I open my eyes to find all three boys sitting on the stairs, watching. "Man she's stubborn."

"I think she gets that from junior, here," Dallas says in jest.

"Not likely, fucknuts," Carson responds.

"Welcome home," I say to Roger, rolling my eyes. "You guys shouldn't be listening in on other people's conversation."

"Hey, I only came down to look for the pizza," Dallas says.

I look at him apologetically and he gives me an annoyed look. "There's no pizza, is there?"

"I forgot, I'm sorry."

"There's no food? Why do I even live here?" Carson asks as they make their way back upstairs. "Is there someone we can call? Children's Aid or Meals on Wheels?"

I laugh once, then turn my attention back to Roger. "Not much has changed."

He smiles and his eyes light up. "I don't want anything to change."

Mischief takes over his expression. I know all about the naughty thoughts that lurk behind that boyish grin. Stepping forward, he traps me between his muscular body and the dining room table. He lifts me to sit and forces my knees apart to accept the width of his hips.

Eyes locked, souls tangled, and hearts reunited. He owns me with a long slow kiss, and his exchange of breath brings me back to life.

"I love you," he whispers.

"I know," I say, moving his hand to my heart. "I can feel it, right here. I love you, too."

"I don't just want fucking. I want kissing. I want cuddling. I want feelings."

"Ugh, the **F**-word."

"I want us to have a great big, blended family. I want to make babies of our own." He kisses me on the forehead. "No more running. No giving up. I promise you, Victoria, I'm not going to let us expire. This guy here..." he taps himself on the chest, "...isn't going anywhere."

Epilogue

A year later, I drive the ZL1 through the dirt parking area and find a spot in the shade of a large oak tree. I sneeze as I walk through the freshly cut grass.

Stunned, I stand in front of the large marble monument that's been placed on my dad's grave.

Stanley Campbell - Loving husband and father.

My breath catches.

"It's wonderful," A female voice says from behind me.

"Hi, Mom." I look past her to see her husband leaning against the car. It takes me a moment but I'm learning to let go. I acknowledge him with a small wave.

"Did you do this?" I ask curiously.

"No. I got an email from the cemetery caretaker saying there was some kind of dedication going on here today.

I scrunch up my face. "That's odd. So did I."

"You mean you didn't do it either?"

"Nope." I lean down to place a bouquet of flowers at the base of the marker and read the garden tag that's hanging on a freshly planted blueberry bush. "But I think I know who did."

A familiar van pulls in and travels along the dirt trail to the back of the cemetery. The boys jump out and head across the grass toward us. Tanner scoops up Molly and places her on his shoulders. She squeals and laughs when he starts to run.

"Gramma!" He throws his arms around my mother, making Molly giggle when he nearly dumps her on the ground.

Roger arrives at my side, brimming with excitement.

He hands my mother the squirming three-month old that he's carrying. "Here, take your granddaughter."

She settles once she's in her arms. "She's gorgeous."

"Roger makes beautiful little girls," I agree.

"She looks just like you."

"She's just as stubborn," Roger adds.

Bill hesitantly joins us. "It's nice to see you again," I say, trying to put him at ease.

Molly inches her way over to my mom and slowly reaches up to take her hand. Mom looks down at her and smiles.

"I planted blueberries for Grampa Stan."

"You did?"

She nods, excitedly.

"He loves blueberries."

"Yeah, but he's dead," she says, matter-of-fact. "So Chloe and I will have to eat them."

I glance over at Roger, trying not to laugh. She's just like her father.

My mother smoothes her hand over Molly's hair. "I'm fairly certain that he'd be okay with that."

I smile. "I think so, too. Just watch out for bears."

Roger laughs at Molly's expression. "Would you and Bill like to come back to our place for dinner?" Roger asks.

"Oh, I don't think so," my mom says, looking uncomfortable. "We don't want to impose."

Roger places his hand on the small of my back and rubs it gently. "It's not an imposition at all, Mom. We'd love to have you."

"Hey, Gramma," Carson starts as he walks back to the car. "Can I come live with you?"

"You want to live with me?" she asks shocked.

"Yeah, since Roger moved in, all I hear all night is sex noises."

Roger bursts out laughing.

"Carson!" I object.

"Well, what makes you think it'll be any different at my house?" She winks and gives Bill a playful slap on the ass.

Carson's mouth hangs opens in disgust. "That's disturbing. I hope you guys are happy now, I'm scarred for life."

My mom and I share an amused look. "Great then," she says smiling. "Our job here is done."

The Headwaters

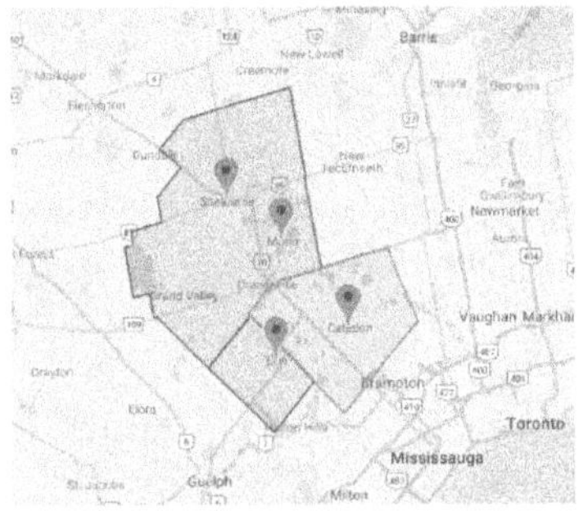

The Town of Orangeville
Historic Charm, Dynamic

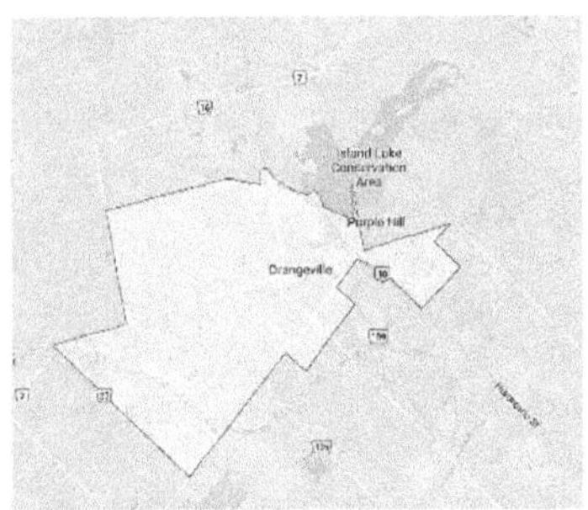

Future

See everything this beautiful countryside has to offer on the online Headwaters Visitor Guide at Headwaters.ca

There is no place more beautiful to me than the home I've made with the love of my life. We're surrounded by rushing waters, rugged landscapes, rolling hills and magnificent views. Where people are real, and life doesn't have to be perfect to be wonderful. It's the most magnificent inspiration for love. Set in the communities that form the Headwaters, the 'Love in the Hills of the Headwaters Series' will bring you stories you can relate to; people you can connect with; and love you can believe in. It's the perfect place for city glam to meet country charm. Come Join us in the Hills of the Headwaters and find a place to explore, unplug and fall in love.

BEHIND THE Tangerine Door

Love in the Hills of the Headwaters Series — Book One

'Behind the Tangerine Door' there was mystery, there was tragedy, and there was love. Journey home to Mono Mills with Cora Scott and uncover the secrets her grandparents kept for many years. While you're visiting, try not to fall in love with Ben, he's not your typical boy next door. His bossy nature and sarcastic sense of humour will challenge you at every turn. Home with family is where he belongs, and he'll never leave the hills of the headwaters. When sentimental childhood memories and international career opportunities collide, Cora is left with the difficult decision of pursuing her dreams or following her heart.